Herdlands

Plai

acepride Territory

Valley

g Tree

Vulture Pool

CURSE OF THE SANDTONGUE

BRAVELANDS

BLOOD ON THE
PLAINS

BRAVELANDS

CURSE OF THE SANDTONGUE

BRAVELANDS

BLOOD ON THE
PLAINS

ERIN
HUNTER

HARPER
An Imprint of HarperCollins*Publishers*

Library of Congress Cataloging-in-Publication Data
Names: Hunter, Erin, author.
Title: Blood on the plains / Erin Hunter.
Description: First edition. | New York : Harper, [2022] | Series: Bravelands: curse of the
   sandtongue ; #3 | Audience: Ages 8-12. | Audience: Grades 4-6. | Summary: "Grandmother's
   attacks on the creatures of Bravelands come to a head"— Provided by publisher.
Identifiers: LCCN 2022021873 | ISBN 978-0-06-296692-6 (hardcover)
Subjects: CYAC: Animals—Fiction. | Adventure and adventurers—Fiction. | Africa—Fiction. |
   LCGFT: Animal fiction.
Classification: LCC PZ7.H916625 Blr 2022 | DDC [Fic]—dc23
LC record available at https://lccn.loc.gov/2022021873

Typography by Ellice M. Lee
22 23 24 25 26   PC/LSCH   10 9 8 7 6 5 4 3 2 1
❖
First Edition

CURSE OF THE SANDTONGUE

BRAVELANDS

BLOOD ON THE PLAINS

PROLOGUE

Windrider's bones creaked as she spread her wings and took to the sky. Her feathers were thinning, but they still bore her aloft on the warm thermals over Bravelands. From high above, the plains and forests and watering holes looked just the same as they always had, the movement of herds and flocks of birds no different from any other day. But as she circled lower, she began to hear hooting and keening from the animals, and to see patterns of movement as individuals and small groups peeled away and headed for the Great Father's clearing.

Young Stormrider soared beside her. Her great-great-grandchick was strong and graceful, her fledgling's dark neck feathers completely covered now in adult white. But she still had a lot to learn about the life of Bravelands. Stormrider flapped anxiously in circles, looking from Windrider to the mourning creatures down below.

"But what if it *is* like last time?" Stormrider asked again as they circled once more around the Great Father's clearing, the figures of the gathered animals below growing larger and smaller as they dipped toward the ground and then banked away again into the sky. "What if there's no Great Parent for a long while? The longer the Great Spirit is gone, the more danger Bravelands is in—you taught me that. What if another False Parent tries to take over? What if . . ."

"Patience, chick," croaked Windrider. "The Great Spirit has not left us. The new Great Parent will be found when the time is right."

The wind ruffled Stormrider's feathers as she briefly drifted against the thermals, before she caught the calmer air and bobbed alongside Windrider once more.

"Do you know the history of the Great Spirit?" Windrider asked.

Stormrider cast her a frown. "I know that it's always chosen one creature to lead the others . . . that they get to speak sky-tongue and sandtongue, and . . ."

"I mean the beginning of it all," Windrider said. She shook her head. What were the mothers thinking these days, if they didn't educate their chicks? "Let me tell you the old story. It's almost the oldest story, and it begins with an egg."

"A vulture egg?"

"No," said Windrider. "But a vulture found it. It was all alone on the plains, not in a nest, not even in a hole in the ground. To the vulture, it looked like a tasty snack. But just as she was about to spear the egg with her beak, she heard a voice speaking to her. *Do not eat this egg*, it said. *Instead, take it back to your nest, and care for it as if it is your own.* So she did. The other vultures laughed at her, sitting on an egg that wasn't hers. They said she was going to hatch a snake or a lizard that would bite her as soon as it was born. But she persisted, staying with the egg until it hatched."

"And what was it?" Stormrider asked, her eyes wide.

"Nothing," said Windrider. "The egg was empty. There was nothing at all inside."

". . . But there wasn't *really* nothing, was there?" Stormrider pressed.

Windrider gave a small nod of satisfaction. Perhaps this chick did understand some things. She banked a little, leading them both up higher, until she could see the mountainside where the vulture pool glistened among the rocks.

"No, indeed. What was inside the egg wasn't visible, but it was very real. The Great Spirit was born that day, and it lived not in the world, but in that vulture's heart. She was the first Great Mother. And though the Spirit has passed on to all sorts of other animals, that's why we have a special connection to the Great Spirit."

"Wow," Stormrider said. They flew in silence for a moment, and then the younger vulture flapped thoughtfully and said, "Windrider, if the Great Spirit was what hatched . . . who laid the egg? Who told the vulture not to eat it?"

"An excellent question," said Windrider. She chuckled to herself, recalling the time many, many moons ago when she'd first heard this story as a fluffy, white-feathered chick in her mother's nest. She had asked what would happen if the vulture *had* eaten the Great Spirit. . . .

"And? What's the answer?" Stormrider prompted.

"Oh, nobody knows," said Windrider. "Perhaps the Great Spirit laid itself, somehow. Perhaps it was something else. Nobody knows which came first, the Spirit or the egg. The point is that the Great Spirit hasn't deserted Bravelands in all that time, no matter what, and we must be patient and wait for it to choose its next Great Parent. It chooses the one who can best nurture and protect it."

"Something strong, like an elephant," muttered Stormrider.

"Often so," replied Windrider, "but sometimes the choice is not so obvious. Even the meekest-looking creatures can have great strength in their hearts."

They flew in silence for a while, circling the pool and then heading higher. They flew toward the great mountain, its lower slopes wreathed in fog, the higher ones green and thick with huge trees.

"The air feels strange on the mountain," said Stormrider. "It seems to . . . *shake*. I can taste its smoky breath. What does it mean?"

"I've sensed it too," said Windrider with a sigh. "Something terrible is coming. A great struggle. A war between Earth and Sky. The Great Spirit must be strong, if balance is to return to Bravelands. Let us hope that the new Great Parent is as brave and kind as Great Father Thorn was."

Stormrider gave a shudder, wheeling away from the mountain.

Windrider took a deep breath. She could taste the faint tang of smoke, even from this distance. She held it on her tongue, as she would the meat of a dead creature, and the knowledge came into her heart the same way it always did, quietly and simply.

My death is coming. It travels on this wind.

She banked to follow Stormrider. Her wings were heavy, and the air crept through her thinning feathers and chilled her heart, but she was still strong enough to catch up with the young vulture.

"Peace must come," she said. "But I do not expect to see it."

Stormrider cast a frightened look at her and opened her beak to squawk in alarm, but Windrider cut her off.

"The future of the vultures will be in your talons. Come, let us go back to the roost. I have much to tell you, and it seems it cannot wait. . . ."

CHAPTER ONE

Chase Born of Prowl slunk across the clearing, between the stamping feet of the gorillas. They formed a wall of dark fur and flesh, blocking off her escape, trapping her in the middle of the circle, a single leopard among hundreds of gorillas and dozens of hissing snakes. The closest snake raised its head from its coiled position on the ground and fixed its black eyes on Chase.

The gorillas huffed and pounded their chests in time with their stomping, and Chase's heart pounded in the same rhythm, her fur twitching. Her tail lashed as if it had a mind of its own. The branches of the jungle shook with the thumping of the gorillas' feet, and pieces of leaf and dust drifted down around her.

She had been through this ritual a dozen times, and it never became any easier to force herself to submit. She stumbled and fell to her belly, not lifting her gaze from the staring eyes of the swaying snake, though every remaining instinct in her body was screaming at her to run.

Chase's paws trembled as she dragged herself closer. Could the snake hear her thoughts, as she could hear Grandmother's?

Do it, she thought. *Just do it. I can't bear this. . . .*

The snake struck. Every time, Chase thought that *this time* she was ready for it, and every time she was wrong. The snakes moved faster than she could follow, startling her into a yowl that cut off as the snake's fangs found her shoulder and the venom throbbed through her blood. Everything slowed for a moment, the cries of the gorillas melding into one low roar, until it all snapped back as the second snake bit down on Chase's paw. Fangs sank into her tail, her flank. She twitched, her back legs kicking uncontrollably as each snake delivered its burst of venom.

The gorillas howled and beat their chests in triumph. The circle of them swayed and spun around Chase's pounding head. She thought she saw their jaws dropping unnaturally wide to show dripping snakelike fangs, heads swelling as they leaned over her, silhouetted against the reddened sky. There seemed to be thousands of them.

Something seized her back legs and dragged her out of the circle of snakes. It was another gorilla, one of the young males they called blackbacks, who laid a half-gentle hand on the top of her head.

"Listen for Grandmother's voice," he grunted. "She will end the pain."

Chase managed to nod, and the gorilla went back to the circle as a female, a Goldback, stepped into the middle and held out her hands to accept the snakebites.

Panting with agony and unsteady on her paws, Chase pushed herself up and wobbled away from the gorillas to slump down in a heap, in a dark corner of the jungle, shrouded by leaves and vines.

I'm not safe. Nowhere's safe.

The venom was already doing its painful work, forcing her mind to open to the words of the great snake. The voice of Grandmother never completely left her, not anymore. Between the rituals, she could hear it as a faint hiss in the back of her mind, like the distant sound of the waterfall. With the venom strong and fresh in her veins, she could make out words, mantras, instructions. And if she didn't find a way to stop it, soon she would be just like the gorillas: completely under Grandmother's control.

There were more of them than there had been, more than there should ever be in a normal gorilla troop. Bit by bit, Burbark's gorillas had conquered the mountain, dragging unsuspecting gorillas in to subject them to the venom and force them to accept Grandmother's "gift." Hundreds of gorillas, from huge Silverbacks who screamed and fought until they were finally overwhelmed to young cubs who clung to their mothers' fur as the snakes curled around their tiny bodies and nipped at their chubby legs. They moved across the mountain, stripping the vegetation for their food and their nests.

So much for us leopards being the fiery wrath of the mountain, sent to stop the gorillas taking over, Chase thought, remembering the ancient story her mother had told her of the leopards' origins. *Have I failed the Great Spirit? Have I failed my kin?*

But no. She hadn't failed them—not yet. Not as long as she could keep her own mind and shut out the urge to follow Grandmother blindly into destroying Bravelands. And to do that, she had to get up, ignore the pain and the growing voice in her head, and hurry to find the only remedy for the mental poison: decaying, horrible rot-meat. Every day that her mind remained her own, Chase knew she owed it all to the hyena Ribsnapper, who'd told her that the hyenas had found the secret to evading the sandtongue curse.

She had to reach the trees by the river, at the edge of the gorillas' original territory. It was a long way to go while her paws still twitched unexpectedly and she couldn't walk in a straight line, but it was the only way to be safe. . . .

"Chase," said a voice, and she jumped and looked up into the hazy face of a gorilla, a Goldback whose name she didn't recall. Chase tensed. "Is Burbark at the ritual?"

Chase blinked, trying to stop the gorilla from swimming back and forth in front of her.

"No," she croaked. "He must be in the caves."

The Silverback leader of the gorillas, Burbark, hardly ever attended the rituals anymore. He had plenty of enforcers to make sure they went smoothly, and Chase suspected he was getting his own venom from another, more potent source. As more time passed since the death of the Great Father—at least,

that was what Grandmother claimed had happened; Chase
still held out hope that she was lying, or somehow mistaken—
Burbark was spending whole days in Grandmother's company.
They lurked in the vents below the mountain peak. What
were they talking about in there? What were Grandmother's
plans?

Blood will flood the plains, whispered Grandmother's voice in
her head.

"Blood will flood the plains," muttered the Goldback, and
Chase echoed it back to her.

"I have to hunt," she muttered, and slunk away. The Goldback didn't challenge her.

When she reached the river, she plunged her muzzle into it
for a moment before shaking her head, sending droplets spinning through the air. She lapped up some of the cool, fresh
water, but she knew the relief it gave her wouldn't last. She had
to get to the waterfall. . . .

At last, she heard rustling in the trees, just audible above
the splashing of the water, and looked up to see a pair of eyes
blinking down at her from a patch of darkness.

Thank the Great Spirit, she thought. *He's here.*

Shadow, the black leopard, moved his tail aside to reveal
a second, smaller shape huddled against his side in the tree
branch. Chase's heart swelled as she looked up into the eyes of
Seek, her aunt's orphaned cub—*her* cub now.

He looked very different from the last time she'd seen him.
The bitter sneer was gone from his face, his eyes were bright
again and his fur sleek and well groomed. He was safe. He

was cured. His tail lashed with excitement as he saw her, but then his ears slowly flattened and he dug his claws into the tree branch.

Both the other leopards were looking down at her with concern in their shining yellow eyes, and Chase was suddenly painfully aware of how she must look. Skinny, her fur ruffled and ungroomed, her steps unsteady and shuffling, her eyes bloodshot. She probably seemed like she was half-dead.

Shadow moved, and something tumbled from the tree branch and landed in the leaves on the ground, with a soft and squishy *thump*. Chase's stomach turned as she approached the hunk of impala and saw that it was truly rot-meat—a sheen of some whitish substance covered its exposed flesh, and a maggot crawled from underneath the skin. Chase retched, but she had no choice. Time and repetition had proved Ribsnapper and the hyenas right: consuming this stuff was the only thing that would push Grandmother's influence out of her mind.

She ate, tearing off small pieces and swallowing as quickly as she could. She focused on getting it down and keeping it down, on not regurgitating any of the slick and nasty stuff, until she finally began to feel better, despite the repulsiveness of the food itself. The dizziness faded, and she felt strength return to her paws. She forced herself to finish the meal before looking up, and when she did, Seek and Shadow were both descending from the tree. Seek ran to her and pressed his head under her chin, and she rubbed her face against his.

"Are you all right?" he mewled. "You look awful!"

Chase laughed. He could still be a little blunt, even though now he was no longer full of Grandmother's bile. "Thanks! I'm better now."

"You're not," said Shadow. He was standing back, watching her with those steady yellow eyes. "This has gone on too long, Chase. The plan was to rescue Seek, and we've done that. Come away with us, right now. We can outrun the gorillas if they try to chase us. We'll find fresh territory on the other side of the mountain. . . ."

Chase sighed. It wasn't the first time he'd asked her to run away, and every time he did, it became harder to refuse. But she still shook her head.

"Burbark and Grandmother are plotting something," she said. "I know they are. If I leave, no one in all Bravelands will know what it is until it's too late. She killed my mother, Shadow. She wants to destroy the Great Spirit, and I think she might succeed!"

"But what if they catch you?" asked Seek, looking up at her with huge eyes. "What if the snake decides to *eat* you, like it ate Range?"

Chase shot a disapproving look at Shadow. She'd told him not to tell Seek about Range's death—about seeing him dragged away by the back legs, swallowed down until he was just a lump in the enormous snake's throat. It had been a relief when his back had broken and he had died before the final swallow. . . .

Shadow shrugged. "He had Grandmother in his head for days," he said. "He already knew."

"What if you can't shake off the poison next time?" Seek

said. "I've felt it myself, remember? I know what it's like. . . ."

Chase let out a weary breath.

"I'm much too smart to get eaten," she reassured Seek. "And if I can keep getting rot-meat, I'm sure I'll—"

She broke off. Something was moving in the trees.

"Run," she said, before she even knew what it was. "Some-one's coming."

Shadow and Seek didn't stick around to say goodbye. Just like they'd agreed when they'd first brought the rot-meat to her, danger was here, and so they ran, side by side into the undergrowth, vanishing from sight.

Chase ran to the riverside and put down her head to drink, just as she scented the gorillas. A moment later, Blackbacks shambled into view. A gorilla patrol, heading past on their way around the mountain—she wasn't sure where they were going, but they paused to stare at her with their bloodshot eyes before turning away, recognizing her as one of their own. Or at least, as a creature who wasn't a threat, for now.

Chase gave a shudder, imagining what could happen to Shadow and Seek if the gorillas captured them.

That was too close. Shadow's right. I can't keep this up forever. . . .

CHAPTER TWO

Bramble entered the Great Father's clearing just as dawn peeked over
the treetops and the sunlight fell on the neat pile of leaves and
flowers that covered the body of Great Father Thorn. Animals had been arriving steadily through the day and night,
coming to pay their respects or just to see the Great Father's
fallen body for themselves. There were meerkats and cheetahs
and dik-diks sleeping between the old tree stumps, monkeys
and civets talking in low voices around the edges of the clearing, a black rhinoceros kneeling beside Thorn's body, her
massive horn gently touching the ground as she muttered her
goodbyes.

Bramble carried his armful of fresh foliage over to Mud,
who sat at the head of Thorn's grave, quietly staring at the sky.
He had hardly moved ever since his friend had passed away,
except to fetch more leaves for Thorn, or when his Starleaf

apprentice, Moth, insisted he had to sleep. The elderly baboon looked up and gave Bramble a tired smile when he saw that he'd brought a fresh covering for the Great Father. He nodded, wordlessly, and Bramble began to cover the wilting leaves with a layer of vivid green and flame red flowers.

When he was done, Bramble walked away, not wanting to crowd Thorn, or to be in the way of the mourners who were still coming to pay their respects—and to ask where the new Great Parent was, and what would happen now.

What will happen now?

The question felt like it had been following Bramble ever since Thorn's death, maybe even before that, as close to his heels as his own shadow.

He found himself following the same path into the trees that he'd walked dozens of times in the last day. As he did, he turned the question over and over in his mind, as if it was a tough nut that he could open if he just kept feeling for the ridge where it would crack.

Moonflower and I came here because Dayflower Mistback read it in the Spirit Mouth. The message was clear: evil spreads from the mountain, unless wisdom stands in its path. I thought all we had to do was warn the Great Father, and he would know how to stop it.

He pushed through a dry, crackling bush, following the slight indentation that showed where baboons and gorillas had passed before, and found himself looking down at the secret that Mud was keeping, for now, from the rest of Bravelands.

The snakeskin was still as huge, still as horrifyingly perfect, as it had been when he had dragged it out of the tunnels beneath the plains. A ghostly, translucent form, longer than a tree from end to end and wide enough that a baboon could easily have climbed inside.

The evil was already here. Grandmother had been here, right beneath their feet, and had left her skin behind as an awful reminder.

Where was she now, and how could they possibly stop her from conquering all of Bravelands, with her cult of infected lizards and crocodiles and gorillas, when the Great Parent was dead? Every moment, Grandmother tightened her coils around them all.

I was counting on Thorn's wisdom to stand in evil's path, Bramble thought miserably. *Now what do we do? We've delivered our message. Perhaps our part in this is done. But I can't leave them now. . . .*

He sat in the dim hollow for a while, staring in revulsion at the shed skin, and dwelling on his thoughts, until suddenly he heard thumping pawsteps and a trumpeting sound. Snapped out of his gloom, he pushed the twigs back into place behind him and hurried back to the clearing just in time to see the elephant, Sky, duck under a branch and step into the open space.

Mud was standing, looking up at her, seeming smaller than ever in the elephant's looming shadow. From the other side of the clearing, Bramble couldn't hear what they said to each other, but he saw Sky's gaze fall on the heap of leaves and flowers in the middle of the grass. She raised her trunk into the air and let out a great sad bellow, then made her way across the clearing and—carefully and gently nudging aside any small creatures in her path—knelt beside Thorn's body, draping her long trunk over him and closing her eyes. Other elephants had arrived with her, but they kept a respectful distance, standing at the edge of the trees with their gazes lowered.

Bramble also looked away as Sky muttered something under her breath. Then she stood up again and shook herself, her great ears flapping.

"We will bring Thorn's bones to the elephant graveyard," she announced. "The Great Parent will lie with his predecessors, and . . ." Bramble caught a tiny hesitation, as if she was steeling herself. "And with his dear friend and our stalwart companion, Fearless the lion. They will rest there together, until the end of all days."

Bramble knew only a little about the Three Heroes of Bravelands, but he still felt tears stinging his eyes, as Sky ever so gently scooped Thorn's body up in her trunk. Thorn was still wrapped in many layers of greenery, so that there was just barely a glimpse of a brown-furred tail dangling among the vines.

Mud clambered up onto one of the thick tree stumps, with the help of Moth. He sat, watching Sky move toward the other elephants, his shoulders heaving with sighs.

"Are you all right?" said a voice. Bramble turned, recognizing the soft lilt of Prance, the gazelle. She suddenly stood right beside him, looking up at him with her large, dark eyes. Her long black horns tilted as she turned her head to see him. She may have had no shadow, but she could move as quietly as one when she wanted to, despite her kind's long gangly legs and noisy hooves.

"Me? I'm fine," Bramble said, without really thinking.

Prance tilted her head. She didn't say anything, but Bramble felt as if she was looking into his mind.

"I just . . ." Bramble puffed out his cheeks and blew a long breath through his teeth. "I don't know where my place is now. I don't know what to do."

Prance nodded slowly. "I'm a long way from my herd, like you are from your troop," she said. "Both of us are out of place, but I have a feeling we're both exactly where we ought to be. We must trust in the Great Spirit. That's what Thorn would have wanted us to do."

Bramble was a little surprised to find himself nodding along, feeling a little calmer. Prance gave him a very light, friendly tap on the shoulder with her horns, and then walked away, heading over to the group of elephants.

I am far from my troop, Bramble thought. *But not all of my troop. Where is Moonflower?*

He turned away from the sight of the elephants preparing to leave and the grieving animals in the Great Father's clearing. He needed to find his sister.

Moonflower is very wise, he told himself, feeling better all the time. *Moonflower will know what to do.*

CHAPTER THREE

Prance trotted across the open grass field, hope and nervousness mingling in her heart as she walked beside Sky and the other elephants. Sky still held the limp, vine-wrapped body of Thorn gently in her trunk, and Gallant the lion ran at her side. The sun was dipping toward the evening, and the elephants' shadows were long and sharp on the ground. Prance sped up a little so that she could walk alongside the elephants, staying within their shadows. She felt oddly comforted. Apart from the cool of the shade, it almost felt like having one of her own again.

The place on her chest where Thorn had placed his hand, where *something* had passed between them, still felt faintly warm, though.

What did you do? she thought. *Great Father, what have you given me? Could it be the Great Spirit?*

She couldn't be sure. She didn't feel very different. Wouldn't she feel different, if the Great Spirit was inside her?

She'd thought about telling Mud, or Moth, or even Bramble, about the strange journey she'd been on with Thorn in the moments before he'd died. Far from the rambling, poisoned old baboon who had been lying in the den, he'd been clear and thoughtful, and together they had flown across Bravelands in their shadow forms to spy on—and confront—the great snake, Grandmother. And then he had passed something over to Prance, and when she'd woken up back in her body . . . Thorn was dead.

How could she tell the others about that, when they were all busy grieving the Great Father? What if they thought it was her fault that he was dead? What if they thought that she was trying to claim to be his successor, at the worst possible moment?

But a better moment to bring up the strange journey hadn't come, and the warmth in Prance's chest hadn't gone away.

What does it mean if I'm carrying the Great Spirit?

There was the obvious meaning, too big and absurd to grasp, which Prance couldn't bring herself to truly consider. But what if it was something else?

When she'd seen Sky walk into the Great Father's clearing, the solution had burst into her mind all at once. She remembered the tales: when the last elephant Great Mother had died, False Fathers had taken her place, and the Spirit had been without a home for some time, but eventually it had found Sky. She had carried it in her heart until it had finally found its place with Great Father Thorn.

Perhaps she was going through the same thing? Perhaps she just needed to find the next Great Parent and pass the Spirit to them? And if that was the case, the one creature in all of Bravelands who knew what that felt like was Sky.

So she had asked to be allowed to accompany the elephants to the graveyard, hoping that somewhere along the way she would be able to tell Sky everything. Or perhaps she wouldn't even have to: as she hurried along, feeling very small in the shadow of these majestic, lumbering animals, she thought that the Great Spirit might be steering her to the elephants because one of them was the real Great Parent.

Maybe it's Sky!

After all, who better? She was a real hero, and elephants lived so long, she was only just entering her prime. It would make perfect sense!

The longer their little group walked across the plains, the more Prance became convinced that this had to be the answer. She didn't get a chance to speak to Sky privately— they stopped as little as possible, and when they did pause to drink or rest, Sky was mostly talking to the other elephants, or to Gallant, about the route they'd take and the territories they would pass through. Gallant went off ahead a few times to negotiate with nearby prides of lions, herds of buffalo, or packs of hyenas to let them and their precious bundle of vines take a shorter route straight across places where a lone gazelle would have had to either go around or sprint for their lives. She glimpsed the hairy backs and flicking ears of the hyenas watching her from a high ridge as they walked through a small valley, and she was glad that she wasn't by herself.

As they started their ascent into the mountains, the sun was striking the horizon, turning the clouds above into blazing lines of pink and gold. They followed the steep, well-trodden path through the crags to the elephant graveyard. Prance's breath caught as they came to the top of the ridge and the narrow pass opened to reveal a high wall of stone that stretched for as far as she could see on either side. Twisted trees grew up and over it, dry mountain flowers peeking out from between their roots. Through the single wide gap in the stony expanse, she could glimpse lush grass, trees with spreading branches thick with green leaves, and a few soft white spears of bone among the mounds that must contain the bones of Sky's ancestors.

"We should stay outside the graveyard," said Gallant to Prance. "It's a sacred place for the elephants. It's a great honor for Thorn and Fearless to rest here."

A hoarse cry overhead made Prance look up, and Sky followed her gaze to see a vulture circling above.

"Windrider probably sent them," she said. "To see that Thorn was put to rest."

The elephants began to enter the graveyard, but Sky turned, the bundle of vines and leaves seeming tiny in her large trunk. She knelt before Prance and Gallant.

"If you would like to say goodbye," she said, "go ahead."

Prance's heart squeezed hard with grief and gratitude for this unexpected kindness. She tossed her head for Gallant to go first and stood back respectfully as the lion approached

Thorn's body and whispered something to it. He rubbed his cheek briefly against a thin brown paw that was visible between the leaves, then stepped back.

Prance approached, wondering what she could possibly say. Thorn had welcomed her into his presence when she'd been exiled from her own herd, he fought for her when Mud's predictions told him that she would bring them trouble, and he hardly seemed to notice that she had no shadow. He was a kind and funny presence when that had been exactly what she needed.

"Thank you," she whispered, briefly tapped her nose to the paw, and then pulled back.

Sky lumbered to her feet and turned to enter the graveyard, leaving Prance alone with Gallant at the top of the stony slope as the sunset washed over the rocks and the blue sky above started to darken.

At first, Prance and Gallant sat in companionable silence. Prance's thoughts drifted back to Thorn, to everything he had done for her, and she tucked her front hooves underneath her body and told herself that she would do whatever she could to repay him.

Then Gallant spoke, in a voice rough with emotion.

"Prance," he said. "Can I ask you for a favor?"

"Um. Of course," Prance said. "What do you need?" *What can I do to help a big strong lion?*

"Well, I know that you can travel—you know, without moving. You can leave your body and just . . . go out there." He turned to look back down the narrow path, toward a small gap between the rocks where the plains of Bravelands were dimly visible.

Prance took a deep breath. Did he know somehow about her journey with Thorn?

"Would you do that for me now and find my cub? The one who Menace took and renamed Terror." Gallant looked down at his large paws and sighed. "I thought he was dead. Now he's alive, and he doesn't want anything to do with me, but Thorn . . . Thorn told me not to give up on him. I don't want to leave him with Menacepride, but if that's what he wants . . . anyway, I need to know if he's all right. Can you do that? Go out there and find him?"

"Oh, of course!" Prance said again. She wiggled a little bit, settling herself solidly on the rocky ground, and closed her eyes.

Every time she moved from her physical body to her shadow-self, it seemed to become easier. It wasn't quite like simply standing up, more like walking carefully across a precarious stepping-stone path over a rushing river. But after a moment's effort, she unfolded her shadow legs and rose out of her body, leaving it behind. She saw Gallant lay his chin on his paws and sigh.

"I'll be back soon," she said, although she knew he couldn't hear her.

She sprang up onto the rocks, leaping higher than she could possibly have done in her body, and hopped from crag to crag as lightly as a drifting feather. Far below she could see all of Bravelands laid out: thick yellow grass, deep green forests, rivers and watering holes, kopjes and ravines. She turned and looked across at the gorilla mountain, with its dripping, misty jungle slopes. Thin streams of smoke, or steam, rose from its peak. They looked uncomfortably like twisting snakes.

Menacepride, she thought. *Where are you?*

She bounded away into the air. She suspected Menace wouldn't lead her ragtag pride too far from the last place she'd seen them, and sure enough, in a few hoofbeats she seemed to find herself cantering over the forest where Gallant and Moth had saved her from Menace.

The pride was still there. They were lazing in a loose circle, most of them apparently asleep. Prance landed silently just outside the circle. It was strangely nerve-racking to walk between the snoring lions, even though there was nothing they could do to hurt her in this form.

Terror was not asleep. He was sitting up, picking over the bones of some prey.

He was easily the youngest and the healthiest of the pride. Every other lion who followed Menace was mangy, scarred, or simply ill-looking—rejects and exiles from other prides who followed the daughter of Titan because she could keep them fed through cunning and cruelty.

Suddenly, Terror's head turned and his pupils went wide, his lips pulling back to scent the air, as he abruptly focused on something in the grass beside one of the sleeping older males. Terror's haunches tensed and he lowered his chin almost to the ground. He sprang—but he was too late. Prance watched in fear as the snake that had been hiding in the grass reared up and struck at the old lion, who leaped to his feet with a yowl and the energy of a much younger creature.

Terror jumped in and grabbed the snake, tearing it from the other lion's leg and tossing it aside, where it twitched a few times and then lay still. He pounced again and smacked it onto the ground a few times, as if to be certain it was dead.

The rest of the pride were stirring now, some sitting up wide awake and anxious, others snorting in their sleep.

"All right, Mauler?" Terror asked, through the snake dangling from his jaws.

"Just about," said old Mauler. He glared at the dead snake and gave a feeble roar. "I hate these things. Why are there so many of them these days?"

"It's getting worse all the time," said a gravelly female voice. It was Menace. She walked up beside Terror, sniffed at the snake, and pulled a disgusted face. "They'd never normally attack a lion out of the blue. There's nothing in it for them! Something's up, and I don't like it."

"It suits me fine," said Terror, grinning through his mouthful of snake. He settled down and began to tug at the dead sandtongue. "I like the taste. . . ."

Prance had seen enough, for now. She turned away from Terror and found herself back on the rocky path outside the elephant graveyard, traveling the vast distance in just a few hoofbeats.

She closed her eyes and sat down on the gravel, beside her body. When she opened her eyes again, it was her real eyes, and she could feel the stones pressing into the flesh of her legs, and the chill in the air as the setting sun dropped down below the horizon.

She blinked, took a deep breath, and looked over at Gallant. His great yellow forehead was furrowed with hope and worry.

"Your cub is all right," she said, and she saw Gallant's sides sag as he let out a huge sigh. "But he's still with Menacepride, and things are . . . difficult for them, as they are for all of Bravelands."

She was opening her mouth to tell him that his son still had good instincts, that he'd tried to save another lion from a snake, when a slight, rhythmic tremor in the ground caught her attention. She looked up to see the elephants emerging through the great stone wall.

"It is done," Sky said. "Thorn rests among the bones of our ancestors. We will rest here for the night and make our way back down to the others in the morning. Prance, Gallant, you are welcome to stay with us or travel by night, whichever you choose."

"I'd like to stay," said Prance. "I'm quite tired."

It was true, but more than the ache in her bones from the long journey or the weight of traveling so far from her body, she knew that this was her chance. It would be her best opportunity to talk to Sky about the Great Spirit.

The elephants settled down on the ground around the entrance to the graveyard, leaning their great gray heads against it or flopping massively on their sides. Sky sat up tall, one large foot curled beneath her. Prance moved up and sat beside her, clearing her throat so that Sky looked down at her with a quizzical expression.

"Sky, may I ask you a question?" Prance said.

"Of course," said Sky.

"What did it feel like when you were carrying the Great Spirit? Before it found Great Father Thorn?"

Sky took a deep breath and made a thoughtful *hummm* sound low in her chest. "It felt . . . odd, definitely. As if there was something powerful and precious inside me, with me, wherever I went. I felt this strange sense that I was protected, but that it was my job to protect it, too."

"But, how did you know that *you* weren't the Great Parent? How did you know it was meant for someone else?"

"Oh, I wondered." Sky chuckled. She glanced up, and Prance followed her gaze. The vulture was gone, but there were a few birds flitting through the sky. A pair of nightjars alighted on a rock at the top of the path down from the grave-yard and sat watching the elephants curiously with their big, dark eyes. "But it's the birds, you see. And I suppose the sand-tongues, too, though I didn't really try to talk to them. Not all Great Parents have the same talents, but the one thing that unites them is the ability to speak to all the species of Brave-lands. I could never do it, so I realized the Spirit couldn't be meant for me."

"She's right, you know," said one nightjar, ruffling its feathers.

Prance felt a dropping sensation in her stomach, like the feeling of tripping over her own hooves as a young foal while running with the herd, when the world seemed to slow as she tumbled toward the earth.

"You must accept it soon," said the second nightjar. "Bravelands can't wait long."

Then they both took off, fluttering away across the rocks.

Prance looked slowly up at Sky, but the elephant hadn't reacted at all to the birds' voices.

She can't hear them.

Gallant flopped down beside Sky too, startling Prance, and started to groom his mane.

"I just hope the Great Parent is found soon," he said. "The sandtongue threat is too great for us to face without one. Maybe it's a rhino's turn, or even a hippo. I'd like to see that snake try to take down a hippo, I don't care how big she is. . . ."

Sky chuckled at this, and Prance gave a very thin, weak laugh along with her.

How can I tell them? she thought, a little hysterically. *How can I say that instead of an elephant or a hippo or a lion, I think the Great Spirit might have chosen . . . me?*

CHAPTER FOUR

Chase was lying in her small nest at the edge of the clearing, gnawing on the bones of the fresh prey she'd caught to fool the gorillas. She watched the big black creatures move around, sluggish one moment and lashing out at each other or at the air the next. She could hear Grandmother's voice in her head—it was fainter, and Chase couldn't feel the compulsion to obey, but Grandmother was still in there, muttering threats and making wild promises of conquest. Chase pretended to be busy with her prey but kept a keen eye on the gorillas—when they all echoed the snake's words, she did too.

Shadow and Seek were right: she couldn't keep this up for much longer. But how could she leave, when any moment now she might be able to find out Grandmother's plans? If she could just stay long enough to hear *something* useful, then perhaps they could run and get to the Great Father to warn him, before it was too late. . . .

Suddenly, Chase's fur prickled and she realized that something was happening in the clearing—or rather, that *nothing* was happening. At some point, without her noticing, each of the gorillas had come to a stop and was standing, limp and slumped, their heads cocked, listening. Chase had instinctively blocked out Grandmother's voice, but now she listened, and what she heard sent a shiver all the way down her back to the tip of her tail.

My children, Grandmother was saying. *The time has finally arrived. Come to me. Come . . .*

One by one, the gorillas turned and stumbled into the trees, all moving in the same direction. They walked with faltering, rolling steps and in complete silence, except for the crunching of leaves under their heavy feet.

Come!

Chase stared after them for a horrified moment, then staggered to her paws and followed. She had to keep up the pretense that she was under Grandmother's control, just like the others. Her heart rattled against her ribs as she swayed and dragged her tail in the leaves, following the eerie movement of the gorillas as they began to climb the mountain. She knew just where they were going: the cave they called the Spirit Mouth, where Burbark had been hiding with Grandmother for days now. Chase had never been inside, and she never wanted to, so it was a relief when they stopped outside the mouth of the cave. Chase wriggled between the gorillas' thick legs to the front of the group. She needed to hear what was about to happen.

There was movement in the dark of the cave. Chase peered inside, saw the faint shapes of scales, and braced herself to see Grandmother slithering out of the shadows . . . but what actually came out was somehow worse. Burbark emerged, his long arms outstretched, a massive, silvery snakeskin draped across his shoulders, trailing behind him into the darkness.

"Grandmother has been born anew once more!" Burbark called out, in a rasping voice, holding up fistfuls of her skin. He stared up at the sky, his eyes gleaming. All around, the gorillas whooped and thumped their chests. Chase growled, but she didn't take her eyes off Burbark. "I have guarded her as she grew, ever larger, ever more powerful," he declared. "And now, faithful friends, the time has come at last for us to descend. Let the march to the plains begin!"

Now? Chase thought, desperate panic flaring in her heart. *With no preparation, no time for me to get away? What am I going to do?*

The gorillas around her had stopped their wild hooting. It seemed like even through their sandtongue curse, they were as shocked as Chase.

"B-but . . . Burbark . . . ," one young Blackback said. He spoke slowly, as if dragging the words up from somewhere very deep inside himself. "We've always lived on the mountain. What about 'blood pools on the plains'?"

"Grandmother has explained it all to me," said Burbark impatiently. "All these years, we have *misunderstood*. Blood shall pool on the plains—but it will be the blood of our enemies. Anyone who stands in our path."

"What about Kigelia?" muttered an older Goldback, whose

black eyebrows were speckled with gray hairs. "He led us from the plains, generations ago. He turned his back on them." Several of the other gorillas were frowning and nodding. Chase took a slow, careful breath—could it be that Grandmother had gone too far this time, that asking the gorillas to reject the creed they'd followed all their lives would break her curse?

"Kigelia was right to retreat," said Burbark. "But now it is time for us to return, and face what he could not! He never intended us to be here forever. We can reclaim the plains, *purify* them!"

Chase looked up at the doubtful Goldback, trying to keep her face from showing the flicker of hope she felt. Then the Goldback and the other gorillas began to nod, gazes that had been brightening with suspicion turning foggy and unfocused once more. Chase's heart sank.

"With Grandmother by our side, we can bring peace to the plains at last! The bloodthirsty monsters who live there will submit or be destroyed!"

Chase could see it now: the army of gorillas descending on the plains, bringing Grandmother's fury in their clenched fists, and snakes to spread her gift to every creature they couldn't subdue.

Desperate calculations ran through her mind.

How many lions would it take to fight off an army of gorillas? How many gorillas to take down an elephant? How much damage could a rhino or a hippo do if Grandmother got her poison into their veins?

She had to get out of here and tell Shadow and Seek. Perhaps they could warn the Great Father . . . but perhaps it was too late. Maybe Shadow was right, and they could escape to a new territory, just the three of them.

One thing she knew for sure: she would not march with the gorillas. She would slip away, no matter what. . . .

"Chase Born of Prowl, child of Grandmother," said Burbark, and Chase startled before she could control herself. "Grandmother has a special task for you."

Cold horror seemed to crawl up from Chase's paws.

No. No. I won't.

But she was completely surrounded. If she refused now, she would die, and it would not be a quick or easy death.

So she stepped forward, even though her paws felt as heavy as boulders.

I should have gone with Shadow. I'm such a fool. . . .

"What am I to do?" she asked.

"You will personally act as escort and protector for Grandmother on her journey to the plains," said Burbark, and several of the gorillas gasped, casting impressed or jealous glances down at Chase.

"M-me?" she stammered. "But surely a gorilla, or a whole troop—why me? I'm not worthy of such an honor," she added quickly.

"I agree," sneered Burbark. "But you are smaller than any adult gorilla."

Chase frowned, trying to understand what that had to do with it, until Burbark turned and pointed one thick finger into the dark tunnel.

Chase hadn't thought she could feel much worse, but as she

stared into the cave she began to feel as if she might throw up her rot-meat.

Do not be afraid, said Grandmother's voice in her head. *Come to me, Chase. Be my teeth and my claws.*

Chase looked around at the gorillas, gathered three or four deep all around her, and then squeezed her eyes shut.

"I'm coming," she said. She tried to swallow her fear as she padded toward the cave. She had often wondered if Grandmother could sense that she wasn't a true believer—now it seemed she was about to put it to the test.

Perhaps she could tell, and this was just a trick, to get her to walk to her death. The memory of Range's face swam in the darkness before Chase's eyes, his expression twisted in horror and pain as Grandmother swallowed him whole.

If that's my fate, I'd rather take my chances with the gorillas, she thought. *But if I run now, I'll die for sure. . . .*

Burbark clapped a hand on Chase's shoulder, making her jump halfway out of her pelt. He leaned down, making her stagger under his mighty bulk, and muttered in her ear: "Guard our mistress with your life."

Then he pulled away.

Chase nodded, and then with a racing heart she passed under the rocks and left the bright green forest and the whoops of the gorillas behind her. The tunnel squeezed tight and then opened out a little, into a dark, warm cavern. She could barely see a few pawsteps in front of her. For a moment there was no sound but the faint dripping of water from the ceiling. Chase sniffed, but all she could smell was the strange, acrid scent that sometimes came out of the vents. She sneezed as the steam went up her nose, and while her eyes were shut, she felt something tickling her ear. It was a feeling she was horribly familiar with by now. The flickering of a long, forked snake's tongue.

Thank you for coming, my daughter, said Grandmother. *Don't be afraid. Step into the dark and you will find the way. We have a long path to travel together, you and I.*

CHAPTER FIVE

It was quiet in the forest, compared to the low chatter of grief and anxiety that filled Thorn's clearing, even after the elephants had left with his body. Bramble was glad to walk below the green canopy. It almost felt like home, even though the ground was flatter and the air was warmer. . . .

"Look! Another gorilla!" he heard a voice say. It sounded like a baboon, probably one from the troop that Thorn and Mud had been born into. It was followed by a chorus of shushing, so he decided not to look around and find the voice. He understood that he made a strange sight, knuckling through the undergrowth by himself. Anyway, they'd said *another* gorilla, so he must be going the right way.

"What's he doing?" said another baboon voice.

"Nothing much," replied the first. "Hanging around. Eating all our food."

"Why doesn't he go home?" muttered another baboon. "They don't belong here. With their weird swollen heads . . ."

"He looks like he's been stung by bees," said the second baboon again.

Bramble sighed. He could turn and let them know that he'd heard their comments and probably scare them off, if he chose to. But what would be the point? Instead he kept his head down and went back to searching for signs of his sister.

You're not so attractive either, with your spindly arms and legs, and your brightly colored rumps, he thought sourly.

He found Moonflower sitting in the shade of a tall tree, with two baboons by her side: Moth, the young Starleaf, and Spider, Moth's father. Moonflower and Spider were sharing an orange, peeling apart the tough outer skin and the juicy insides, while Moth sat and stared at something on the ground.

As Bramble approached, all three of them looked up and saw him. Moonflower waved him over. Moth frowned slightly and picked up the stones that lay at her feet, muttering something.

"Moth is showing me how her stones work," said Moonflower, as Bramble settled down with his back against a tree trunk. "It's just like watching the Spirit Mouth, except . . . nothing like that at all."

Moth held the stones out in front of her and turned her face to the sky. "Come on," she muttered under her breath. Then she scattered the stones across the earth in front of her and bent over them, her nose almost brushing the ground as she stared intently at the pattern they had made.

Bramble watched her with his heart in his mouth. Would she be able to see the next Great Parent? Or some way to defeat the sandtongues?

He had never understood the way Moonflower, and her mother, Dayflower, had read the patterns of steam from the Spirit Vent. It had always just looked like steam to him. The same seemed to be true of Moth's stones—he squinted and turned his head, hoping that they might have fallen in the shape of an elephant or something, but they were just stones to him.

Moth shook her head. "I can see something in them," she said. "I'm just not sure what it's supposed to be. Mud still has a lot to teach me about being a Starleaf."

"I once spent a season with a tortoise," said Spider, breaking the silence.

Moth looked up and gave her father an exhausted glare, then went back to looking at the stones.

"They don't believe in worrying about the future," Spider went on. "Don't care for much that's not happening to them in the moment. *What will be, will be*, that's their motto. Funny, considering they live so long."

Moonflower sighed. "The gorillas seek guidance from the Great Spirit all the time," she said. "I wish I still had my mother to teach me how to be a real Mistback. I've seen visions in the mist, so I know I inherited her gift. I just wish I was better at understanding them."

Moth gave Moonflower a sympathetic smile. "I know that feeling," she said, and went back to staring at her stones.

Moonflower looked over at Bramble, and her expression changed. For a moment, Bramble wasn't sure why—did he have a fly on his face?—but then Moonflower reached out and patted his shoulder, and he realized that he must be looking as anxious as he felt.

"Can we talk?" he said and tilted his head, doing his best to indicate, *Over there, away from the baboons.*

Moonflower nodded, and together they got up and wandered between the trees, until they had moved far enough away from Moth and Spider that they couldn't make out what they had begun arguing about.

"Are you all right?" Moonflower said. "I know it's tough that the Great Father didn't pick a successor, but . . ." She trailed off, biting her lip, as if deep in thought.

"I'm fine. But I think . . . I don't know. Should we go?" Bramble said, in a rush. "Have we outstayed our welcome on the plains? We don't belong here. Maybe we should go back to the mountain and try to save my father, or . . . or something? I just don't know what we're here for, now that the Great Father's gone."

Moonflower didn't answer for a moment.

"I had another vision," she said, at last.

"When?" Bramble gasped.

"Last night. I looked up, and I saw it in the clouds. They moved just like steam, and covered the stars, and I saw . . . I think I saw Kigelia. It was the rock, not our ancestor—but even though he was made of rock and covered in moss and flowers, I saw him get up, turn around, and start walking toward the plains. He turned his back on the mountain. And I didn't say anything because I don't know what it means, but . . . maybe it means our place is here, for now."

Bramble opened his mouth to ask her what she thought the Great Spirit wanted them to do on the plains, but he had barely made a sound before there was a rustling of twigs and leaves in the tree above them, and he looked up to see Moth leaping through the branches of the trees as if something was chasing her.

"What's got into Moth?" Moonflower asked Spider, as he scrambled up to them and stared after his daughter.

"She had an idea about what the stones were showing her," Spider said. "She didn't say where she was going. . . ."

"Moonflower!" Moth's voice came from up above. "Come and look!"

Moonflower gave Bramble a look of apprehension and began to clamber up the tree after Moth. Bramble didn't want to be left behind, so he headed up after his sister, climbing hand over hand, pushing up over the branches. The gorillas were a lot slower than the young baboon, and up in the canopy the thin trunk of the tree swayed dizzily under their weight. By the time they reached Moth's perch and Bramble stood unsteadily on a bowing branch, she was pointing across the forest, one thin finger wavering.

"Look!" she said. "Is that what I think it is?"

"The Spirit Mouth," Moonflower gasped.

Bramble followed Moth's pointing finger and took a sharp breath of his own. In the far distance, little more than a shadow of darker-colored sky on the horizon, there was the shape of the mountain. And from the top, a small yet distinct stream of something was rising into the sky.

"What does it mean?" he asked Moth.

"I'm not sure," she said.

"I think it means the Spirit Mouth agrees with me," said Moonflower. "This is where we need to be, at least for now."

They watched the steam rise for a moment. Bramble thought it looked oddly dark—the steam in the Spirit Mouth was usually wispy and pale, and he wouldn't have guessed you could possibly see it from this distance. But it was still a comfort, to look back at his home and feel the approval of the Great Spirit. They would stay, and the Spirit would show him how he could help. He was sure it would.

They climbed down, Moth hanging back to keep pace with Moonflower so they could discuss their visions, passing ideas between them as they tried to puzzle out what each detail might mean. Bramble reached the ground first, and as he landed in the soft undergrowth with a hefty thump, he looked up and saw that Spider wasn't alone at the bottom of the tree. Mud was there too, and he looked up at Bramble with a wide-eyed expression.

"Bramble, there you are," he said. "I have been consulting my stones, and I need to talk to you."

That was quick, Bramble thought. *The Spirit has a task for me already?*

"Did you see the smoke from the mountain?" he asked.

"Moonflower and Moth both think it means we need to stay on the plains, at least for now."

Mud smiled. It was the first smile Bramble had seen on the old baboon since Thorn had died, and something about it—and the way Spider was drumming his hands excitedly on the ground just behind Mud—made Bramble's stomach turn over with anticipation.

"That's right," said Mud. "Because the stones have confirmed what I've thought for some time. I have found the next Great Parent—and it's you, Bramble."

Bramble stared blankly at Mud. He suddenly felt as if the baboon was speaking to him from a long, long way away. He rustled in his mind for something to say, but it was as quiet and dark in there as the peak of the mountain on a starless night.

"I—what?" he said at last. "How? Why would it be me?"

"You underestimate yourself," said Mud. "You are a hero, Bramble. The Great Spirit speaks through you; it has ever since you risked everything to come here. You did all you could to save Thorn, but that was never your destiny. The Great Spirit brought you here to be his successor, not his savior."

"*Bramble!*" Moonflower gasped, dropping down beside him with her mouth hanging open. "Did I just hear what I thought I heard?"

She didn't wait for an answer, but threw her arms around him with such force that their heads banged together.

"I . . . I don't know what to say!" Bramble said, his mind

racing as his sister squeezed him tight. *Can I speak to birds? Can I look through the eyes of other creatures, like Thorn did? I don't know—I haven't tried!*

Mud stepped up to him and put a firm, wrinkled hand on his shoulder.

"Say you will serve Bravelands and the Great Spirit," he said. "Say you will lead us through this darkness, to the best of your ability. That's all any Great Father can promise."

Bramble drew himself up, disentangling from Moonflower's arms.

Bravelands needs leadership, desperately, he thought. *I was going to be a Silverback one day—I'm strong, and I'm not afraid. I can shoulder this burden.*

"I promise I'll do my best," he said.

Mud clasped his hands, and the forest echoed with the sound of Spider's joyous whooping.

CHAPTER SIX

Prance walked ahead of the elephants, the comforting rumble of their footsteps following her across the plains. Gallant kept pace beside her. They had started the journey back to the Great Parent's clearing in the early morning: mist lingered in the hollows and rolled across the horizon, though the sky was clear. Later on, the sun would beat down remorselessly on any creature caught out of the shade, but for now it was cool and quiet.

At least, Prance could tell that it *would* have been quiet, if it hadn't been for the chatter of the birds. Some circled above, and others landed nearby. One bright red fledgling songbird even landed on her horns.

"Good morning, Great Mother!" it chirruped. "Are you going to the watering hole? Are you going to deal with the snakes? Is it true you can see through our shadows? The sparrows said that the nightjars said that the vultures said . . ."

"Chichi, stop pestering the Great Mother!" said a larger songbird, flapping around Prance's horns until the young bird let out a *chirrup* of apology and fluttered off.

"Good morning!" chorused a flock of spurfowl, running alongside Prance for a moment, bobbing their bright orange faces before vanishing into the grass.

"Congratulations, Great Mother," called out a small group of sunbirds as Prance and Gallant passed by a small copse of trees. One of them ruffled his iridescent neck feathers. "And congratulations to your herd!" he added.

"You know you'll have to tell your friends at some point, don't you?" said a rather smug starling from the next tree along.

Prance simply sighed.

They were right, of course. Any doubts she'd had before about whether she'd dreamed the conversation with the nightjars had been banished as soon as they started walking.

I'm no custodian. I . . . I am the next Great Mother.

She went a little farther in silence, listening to the chatter of the birds, until she spied a small watering hole up ahead.

"Let's pause for a drink," she said to Gallant. "I know we haven't been walking long, but I'm thirsty."

The two of them reached the water first and bent their heads to drink while the elephants caught up. Prance thought about how strange this sight must be to any creature who didn't know them—a lone gazelle, drinking beside a lion without so much as a nervous glance in his direction.

She hoped that each gulp of water would clear her throat and make it easier to say what she had to say, but no matter how much she drank, it was hard to begin.

"Gallant," she said, and her voice came out as an undignified squeak. *Not very Great Motherly!* "I have something important to say," she went on. She raised her head to look at him and saw him staring back at her . . . with an expression of wide-eyed, lip-curling anger. Prance's hooves skittered under her and she backed away, terror seizing her before she could even think to be confused. At that moment, Gallant sprang forward, but as she braced herself to feel his teeth close in her throat, he veered around her, his paws splashing through the water's edge, and he pounced on something behind her with a low growl.

Prance almost tripped over her own legs as she turned and saw Gallant straddling the back of a crocodile, pinning it with its jaws under water, its yellow eyes wide and its tail thrashing.

"Run, Prance!" said Gallant.

Prance began to back away.

"No, wait," said a strangled, bubbling voice, and Prance felt a shiver run from the base of her horns down to her tail. It was the crocodile. Of course: she could understand sandtongue, too. She stared at the creature, realizing with shock that she could read the fear in its eyes. "Please, don't kill me!" it said, through a mouthful of water. "I'm not cursed!"

"Wait, Gallant," Prance said. "Don't hurt it." She stepped gingerly closer to the crocodile.

"What are you doing?" Gallant snarled. "Stay back, Prance!"

Prance lowered her head and bent her knees so she was closer to the eye level of the crocodile, though she still stayed at least a full gazelle-length away. "If he lets you go, you won't try to bite us?"

"No!" said the crocodile. "I'm just looking for my father, and I thought you could help!"

"Then prove it to us," said Prance. "Stop struggling."

The crocodile's tail swished through the water once more, sending up spray, and then it seemed to take in a deep breath through its nostrils and go still.

"Good," Prance said. "Gallant, I think you can let it go."

"What are you talking about?" Gallant frowned at Prance and then at the crocodile. "How did you do that? Tell it to stop like that? What in Bravelands is going on?"

Prance almost laughed. When she'd imagined telling Gallant her news, this wasn't quite what she'd pictured.

"Please," she said.

Gallant growled, and Prance could see the worry in his face as his eyes flickered from her down to the crocodile and back. "Well . . . all right," muttered Gallant, after a long pause. "But if you're wrong, don't blame me."

With a snort and a toss of his mane, he stepped back off the crocodile's spine and out of the water.

The crocodile took two steps up onto the bank, until Gallant growled deep in his chest, and then stopped.

"Thank you," the crocodile said. "I'm sorry, I really didn't mean to sneak up on you. I'm just looking for my father. I wondered if you knew him."

"I—I don't know any crocodiles," Prance said. "I'm sorry."

"Oh, he's not a crocodile," said the creature. "He's a baboon called Spider."

Prance stared at it for a moment. "Your . . . father is Spider?" She found herself trying to think what Spider's troop name was, to make sure he was talking about the same baboon— then she shook herself. What other Spider could possibly have adopted a crocodile?

"*Excuse me?*" said Gallant. "Prance, are you certain you haven't been sitting too long in the sun?"

"It's a long story," said the crocodile. "But that's why I thought you might know him. I need to tell him about the rest of the bask. They're cursed!"

Prance shuddered a little. "Was it like they were suddenly different animals?"

"Yes!" said the crocodile.

Prance remembered the giraffe leader who had been bitten by snakes, and the strange, violent behavior that creatures had been reporting to Great Father Thorn for days. She remembered the giraffe staring at the mountain as he told her he would lead his herd in a pointless war against the hyenas. . . .

"Was it like they could hear a voice in their heads that you couldn't?"

"That's exactly it!" said the crocodile. "They all just left one day and started walking, all at once! Crocodiles don't do much together," it added. "It was spooky. I tried to stop one of them and nearly got my nose bitten off for my trouble. I need to tell Spider—he'll know what's happening."

"I'm afraid you're right," Prance said. "They are cursed—"

"Prance," Gallant interrupted. "How are you doing this? You're talking like you can understand it, but nothing you're saying makes sense!"

Prance looked at him and took a deep, steadying breath. "I can understand him," she said.

"But . . . how? The only grasstongue creature who can speak sandtongue is the Great Parent!"

Prance waited for the light of understanding to come into Gallant's eyes, but he kept looking back and forth between her and the crocodile, as if there was no conceivable explanation for what was happening in front of him. She smiled.

"Gallant," she said in a gentle voice. "You know how I said I had something important to tell you? Well . . . this is it. I can speak sandtongue. I can speak skytongue, too. I didn't know it myself until last night—I couldn't accept it could really be me, but . . ."

Finally, Gallant's amber eyes went wide, his ears flicked back in surprise.

"Great Mother!" cried a small voice, and Prance looked up just in time to brace herself as a flock of weaver birds came hurtling out of the sky, circled around her horns, and then landed on the ground all around her, chirping and hopping anxiously. "Great Mother, Great Mother!" they said.

"What's the matter?" Prance asked.

"It's terrible, terrible!" said one of the weavers.

"We came quick! We wanted to warn you!"

Prance saw Gallant's wide eyes flicker as he took in the

fluttering flock of birds. Then she glanced up and saw with a jolt that more birds were flapping and bobbing toward them— soaring vultures, yellow-necked lovebirds, starlings, and even an ibis with a long, pointed beak.

"There's a terrible mistake being made at the clearing!" said one of the weavers.

"Mud's got the wrong one!" panted another.

"The wrong what?" Prance asked.

"The wrong Great Parent!"

"It's a gorilla," said a weaver. "He's going to anoint a gorilla as Great Father, instead of you. You have to hurry!"

Prance's heart sank.

What happens if the wrong Great Parent is anointed? Maybe nothing. Maybe something awful . . .

She looked up at Gallant. "I'm the Great Mother," she said. "And I have to go. Tell Sky, and then . . . try to keep up."

And with a toss of her head and a flick of her tail she sprang over the small birds and broke into a run, pounding across the plains, the birds wheeling around to soar behind her, trailing across the sky like a shadow.

CHAPTER SEVEN

Chase squinted into the darkness. Her eyes were starting to adjust, and she could make out shapes of darker black against the deep gray. Were those tunnels? Where did they lead? She thought it was growing hotter in here, and the steam thicker—but it might just have been that panic was settling in her heart, making it harder to breathe.

This way, said the voice of Grandmother.

Parts of the cave—dim shapes that Chase had *thought* were smooth rocks and piles of earth—began to shift around her. Chase shuddered as she realized that they were not stone at all, but parts of Grandmother's enormous body. The snake's head came into view, slowly, the faint light from the entrance to the cave glinting in her black eyes. Her head, by itself, was as large as Chase, and her body lay in thick coils all around them. Was she . . . *even bigger* than she had been last time Chase had seen her? Perhaps it was her imagination.

"Which way, Grandmother?" Chase managed to say.

There, said the snake, and her huge head moved over to point into one of the deep, black holes.

"Where does it go?" Chase asked.

Time to put your trust in me, said Grandmother. *Lead the way, my champion.*

For a moment, Chase wondered just how bad it would be to be consumed by a giant snake or battered to death by gorillas. Was there any chance, any chance at *all*, that if she tried to refuse she could make it back to Shadow and Seek?

No. None.

Survival, then. It was the only way.

Tentatively, she stepped into the tunnel entrance.

The rocks crowded in on all sides, tickling the fur on her ears and shoulders, making her whiskers tremble with the effort of feeling her way through the small space. She hoped that the tunnel would open out again soon. Every step, she imagined it releasing her into a bigger cave, letting her feel like she could breathe in a full breath, and giving her more space to move away from the unmistakably horrible scraping sound of a huge snake following down the tunnel behind her.

But the tunnel went on and on. Twenty steps down a steep slope, fifty—so many that Chase lost count, restarted, and lost count over and over again. Her paws began to shake as she stumbled on, blind as a worm with only her whiskers to guide her.

She was certain now that the air was getting hotter, and

although there was no steam rising through the passages like there had been in the cave, the strange acrid smell was growing stronger. Once or twice, she felt the shape of the tunnel change, and realized that it had split into two, or even more, smaller passages. She paused, and the voice of Grandmother spoke up in her mind: *Left*, or *Turn here*, or *Down, always down for now.*

Eventually, at last, she saw gray shapes in front of her. She blinked, her eyes exhausted from straining in the pitch darkness, and saw that up ahead there was light filtering down into the tunnel from a crack. As she passed underneath it she stopped, craning her neck to try to see out. But she couldn't make out anything but a thin sliver of bright sky.

With a sigh, she carried on, leaving the precious glimpse of light behind. But this time she walked much less far before another one appeared, this one slightly bigger, with a single green trailing vine dripping down into the tunnel.

Even though the tunnel was still painfully dark and it was hard to steer herself down in places, the occasional shaft of light made everything feel much more real—and in a way, that was worse. In the dark, Chase could almost ignore the quiet slithering of snakeskin over rock behind her, but she made the mistake of pausing to look back as she passed by a crack in the tunnel, and there was Grandmother, very real and solid, the red-and-black scales across her huge face gleaming, her red tongue flicking out to taste the air.

I don't think she's planning to eat me, Chase thought as she hurriedly turned back around. *Unless I'm a portable snack—but she could hunt and kill almost anything she chose. So what am I doing here?*

She thought about Shadow and Seek, and her heart squeezed in her chest. Would they see the gorillas leaving the mountain, and what would they think when she wasn't with them?

They would probably think she was dead.

Just keep each other safe . . . she thought. *That's all I want right now. . . .*

"How long is this tunnel?" she said out loud, after a little while longer. "Where is it taking us?"

She heard Grandmother let out a hiss, and briefly thought she'd offended her—but the voice in her head sounded amused.

You might as well try to count the stars, the snake said. *Or measure every tree on the mountain. These tunnels were made by my ancestors, and they are taking us to our destiny.*

"Your ancestors?" In the dark, Chase's imagination ran away with this thought. Were the ancestors smaller, more like normal snakes, or were they vast, even bigger than Grandmother?

Your mothers don't teach you the old stories, said Grandmother. *Once, before any creatures existed in Bravelands, anywhere in the skies or the water or the land, there was only the fire snake. She laid her eggs in the mountain and waited many lifetimes of lesser creatures, curled around them, keeping them safe. When the time was right, the eggs hatched, and a thousand of her children went out to find their homes in the world. They came down from the mountain, burrowing through the earth and streaming over the land. These tunnels are their legacy, dug into the very earth of Bravelands.*

Chase frowned.

Fire snakes? she thought. The story her mother had told her about the first leopards involved fire, too. Could the two stories be different views of the same thing?

"What happened to the fire snakes?" she asked. "They don't exist now, do they?"

Their bodies cooled, said Grandmother. *They grew pelts, legs, wings. They became all the other creatures of Bravelands. At first, all paid homage to their empress, the fire snake who still lived in the mountain. But the truth has been forgotten. Ungrateful animals crawl and stomp and swim across the surface. They have their Great Spirit, but it is nothing compared to the truth.*

You ask where we are going, Grandmother added, and Chase sensed a wry note in the voice inside her head. *We are going to the plains, to bring the truth to the creatures who live there. Before I am done, they will remember their rightful ruler.*

Chase didn't ask what would happen if they refused to bow to Grandmother or declare their allegiance to the great fire snake. Instead she said, "The leopards have a different story, but it's strangely similar. My mother told me that we fell from the sky as flaming rocks. We were sent to defend the mountain from the gorillas," she added, and then winced with regret. Would Grandmother sense the irony of that?

I feel no bitterness, she said. *Ignorance flourishes in weak minds.*

Chase's fear immediately melted back into anger. Grandmother's story was just that—a story. It shouldn't have surprised Chase that the snake would dismiss her kind's stories so easily, when she'd orchestrated so much real misery—but somehow it did. She felt a growl start to form in her throat, but then quickly took a breath and tried to stay calm. It would be a very foolish thing to get herself killed over. . . .

Eventually another patch of light appeared up ahead, but this one was different. It was brighter, and Chase found herself stepping out of the mouth of a tunnel into a much larger space—still underground, still definitely a cave, but a cave with room to move and turn around. There was even a pool of water in one corner, a trickle dripping steadily down from above onto a smooth rock. Chase went over to it and began to lap at it gratefully.

She wondered where they were now. Were they still on—or in—the mountain? The sky above was deeper blue, but Chase couldn't guess what that meant.

Rest, said Grandmother. *I must do the same.* She slithered in behind Chase, her huge head just barely fitting through the gap into the cavern. Chase pressed herself to the wall, suddenly wondering whether the whole of the snake would even fit in the space, and how tightly she would be caught in her coils—but Grandmother's head turned and she began to move toward another tunnel exit, one that Chase could just see led into another cavern space, before it was obscured by Grandmother's scales. *Wait here for me, and do not allow anything to disturb my sleep.*

"Yes, Grandmother," Chase said. She waited, lapping at the pool of cool water until the tip of Grandmother's tail had vanished through the entrance and all she could see beyond was darkness. Then she waited a little longer, until any sounds of movement had ceased, and all she could hear was the gentle dripping of water and the very faint sound of breathing.

If she was going to run, she should do it now.

Would it be better to go back the way she came? She knew that somewhere back along this path lay the exit back into the mountain through the Spirit Mouth, less than a day's march away. But how quickly would Grandmother be able to follow her? And even if she didn't, Chase knew she could easily be lost forever, certainly long enough to starve, in the pitch-black tunnels. Running off downhill toward wherever they were headed almost seemed like the smarter option—she *knew* she didn't know where that tunnel went, so she would be exploring with an open mind instead of trying to retrace her steps. And perhaps she'd be able to find another crack in the wall or the ceiling big enough to squeeze through. But if she had to retrace her steps, she would be walking right back into Grandmother's open jaws. Which only left trying to dig her way out—but not here. The rock was too solid, the opening too small, and anyway it would make too much noise.

I'm stuck here, she thought. *With Grandmother. For now.*

She told herself there would be other opportunities. She had to try to believe it. . . .

The shaft of light had crossed the cavern floor and was gleaming from the surface of the pool, when Chase heard stirring from the side chamber and looked up to see Grandmother emerging once again.

She seemed to glisten, her scales seeming brighter and

cleaner than before, the red patterns more vivid against the black. And this time, Chase was certain, she was just a tiny bit larger than she had been before.

"You were . . . shedding?" Chase said.

They're coming more frequently now, said Grandmother. For a moment, she sounded tired. Chase wondered if the process of shedding was difficult for her.

And if so . . . could that be exploited?

Soon, I will be too large to traverse these tunnels, Grandmother went on, seeming to cheer up as more and more of her coils poured into the cavern. *Very soon now, when the sun no longer shines in the daytime, I will reach my final form, and no claw or fang will be able to pierce my scales. I will be invincible then, and the world will tremble beneath my coils.*

Invincible, Chase thought, her heart dropping once more into the pads of her paws. *Then . . . it will be all over for Bravelands. But "when the sun no longer shines in the daytime"—that can't happen, can it?*

Let us move on, said Grandmother. *Take the right fork here.*

"Oh—really?"

Chase had spent a moment or two exploring the ways out of the cavern. There were two that didn't lead back the way they'd come or into the side chamber where Grandmother had shed her skin—the left sloped downward, which she imagined led closer to the plains, and the right sloped slightly up.

The right, Chase.

Chase's whiskers twitched.

"Yes, Grandmother," she said obediently. "Are we going

uphill very far? I thought we were going toward the plains."

Not yet, said Grandmother. *First, we need to take care of an ancient enemy.*

Chase's fur rippled with a shudder. The only ancient enemy she could think of was the Great Father, but he would be on the plains, wouldn't he?

If not him . . . then who?

CHAPTER EIGHT

Am I ready for this?

Bramble hesitated at the edge of the last line of trees before the watering hole, staring across the grassy plain toward the gathered animals. The sight of them all made him catch his breath. Even in the clearing, he had never seen a collection of creatures like this. Predators and prey stood side by side, and huge animals like giraffes and buffalo stood out against the skyline, dwarfing the smaller animals that he knew were clustered around them.

They're all waiting for me, Bramble thought. *I have to do my best.*

"Ready?" Moonflower asked, echoing his thoughts as she walked up beside him.

"I'm not sure it's possible to be ready for this," Bramble said. "But I'm going anyway."

"I'll be right behind you," his sister said.

With a deep breath, he stepped out of the shadows of the trees and into the sunshine. It felt like a long walk, knowing all the while that one by one the animals were noticing him coming, sizing him up, wondering if he was really the Great Father who would lead them to a peaceful future. . . .

As he approached the watering hole, he saw Moth helping Mud up onto a jutting rock that stuck up over the water. Bramble made his way to him, not meeting the eyes of the kudus and mongooses and wildebeests that stepped reverently out of his path.

Mud waved him over, but as Bramble got closer he could see a faintly worried look on the old baboon's face. His stomach clenched with anxiety. Was something wrong already? Was there trouble brewing among the gathered animals? But Mud didn't seem concerned with the creatures on the ground—he kept looking up at the sky, squinting his eyes, peering down at the edge of the watering hole, over at Bramble, and back to the sky again. Bramble followed his gaze and saw there were birds circling overhead, far above the watering hole.

"Ah, Great Father," said Mud as Bramble came to the edge of the rock. "Good, good. You're here."

"Is something the matter?" Bramble asked, looking up at the birds overhead.

"Oh, no, probably nothing," Mud said. "It might just be my old eyes, I can barely see. . . . The birds seem to be staying very high up. But perhaps they're afraid of the sandtongue curse. I daresay if I could avoid walking on the earth right now, I might. Can you hear anything they're saying, Great Father?"

Bramble squinted into the sky. He knew that as the Great Father, he was supposed to be able to understand the voices of birds, as well as snakes and lizards—but surely they were much too far away to hear? He tried to listen as hard as he could, but there was nothing but a few extremely faint cries.

"Is it a problem if they don't come down?" Bramble whispered to Mud.

"No, no," said Mud, in a vague tone of voice that Bramble was afraid might mean yes. "Normally a new Great Parent would use the birds to summon Bravelands to the ceremony—but there's no need. All these creatures were here to pay their respects to Thorn, or they came when they heard the news from the baboons. Word will spread. No, it doesn't matter." He patted Bramble's shoulder with a firm hand, and Bramble was slightly reassured.

At least, until Moonflower stepped closer to him and, under her breath, said, "*Have* you heard any birds talking?"

"Well, no," said Bramble. "But maybe *they* don't know it's me either, yet."

"Hmm," said Moonflower, nodding thoughtfully.

Bramble turned to look around at the animals. Some of them were staring at Mud, waiting for something to happen. Others seemed to be tired of waiting and were dipping their heads to drink listlessly from the watering hole.

Is this a Great Gathering? he thought. It was bizarre. Suddenly, the voice of his father, his mother, all the gorillas, echoed in his mind: *Blood pools on the plains.* But in this moment, hyenas were drinking peacefully beside dik-diks and meerkats. There were even a few lions—members of Gallantpride, he guessed, though Gallant himself was away with the elephants—sitting quietly, their tails twitching. Many of these animals would eat each other in a heartbeat, at any other time.

Mud cleared his throat.

"My friends," he said, raising his arms to the sky. His voice didn't carry very far, and for an awkward moment Bramble thought that none of the animals were going to respond at all. But then Moth gave the wildebeest next to her a hard nudge on the ankle and it snorted, raised its head, and then bellowed.

"Silence for Mud Starleaf!"

The animals fell silent, staring at Mud.

"My friends. Many of you have come here to pay your respects to Great Father Thorn," said Mud. He cleared his throat, trying to speak up, to reach the twitching ears of the creatures all the way on the other side of the watering hole. "Many of you have asked me what happens now, who the Great Spirit has chosen to be the next Great Parent."

"We remember the last time there was no Great Parent!" put in a gnu with a snort. "And back then there was no sand-tongue curse to worry about!"

There was a general muttering of agreement. Mud frowned, looking put out at being interrupted before his speech had really begun, but he raised his chin and held out his hands for quiet.

"The Great Spirit has told me its choice," he said, and that did make all the animals pay attention. "A new host, with the potential to unite Bravelands—grasstongues and skytongues, predators and prey, the plains and the mountains!"

Bramble felt his hands begin to shake. Several of the animals gathered around the watering hole were looking at him now, and the muttering was starting up again. He tried not to look away from their interested, skeptical gazes. He felt less like a Great Parent, and more like an interloper, intruding on a ritual he didn't really understand.

"Maybe this isn't a great idea," Moonflower muttered, as if she could read his mind. "Maybe we should wait a bit. . . ."

"I promised Mud," Bramble whispered back.

Mud slapped his hands against the rock. "Bravelands needs a leader!" he announced. "And the Great Spirit has sent us this gorilla, Bramble, to take Great Father Thorn's place. The Spirit sent me a sign—that the new Great Father would travel a great distance, crossing Bravelands to come to our aid at this moment. I saw Thorn, standing with the sun behind him, casting a long shadow. What creature could be more like the great shadow of a baboon?" he asked, gesturing to Bramble.

Bramble fought back a shiver of unease. Was that really what Mud had to go on? A shadow?

But he refused to let the other animals see his doubt. Whether Mud was right about the vision or not, he was right that Bravelands needed a leader, and Bramble would do his best, no matter what. . . .

"Bramble Blackback," Mud said. "Take your place now in the waters, as your fellow Great Parents have done before you.

Gentle Breeze, would your herd please form an honor guard as the Great Father enters the water?" he said. "No crocodile will disturb the ritual."

A shape in the water rose up, and Bramble realized it was a large hippopotamus. Not the same one that he and Moonflower had mistaken for a rock, but very possibly that hippo's close relative.

Gentle Breeze blew a stream of bubbles from her nose, and her ears twitched. At this silent signal, three more hippos rose from the shallows. They gathered, two to either side of Bramble, and Mud put a hand on Bramble's shoulder.

"It's time," he said. "Thorn said that no matter his doubts, when he waded into the water, he felt the presence of the other Great Parents all around him. Go into the water and call out to the animals. Ask them to accept you."

Bramble took a deep breath and cast a last glance back at Moonflower. Then he stepped into the water, shivering as the chill worked between his toes and up over his ankles, and then his knees, and then his whole lower half. The hippos kept pace with him as he pressed out—how far was he supposed to go?—and the other animals looked on with reverent, interested stares. He looked up and saw the faint shadow of the mountain in the distance.

Bramble Blackback, Great Father, he thought. *Once, I dreamed of being Bramble Silverback, of leading my own troop. I never thought I would lead all of Bravelands! I'm so far from home. . . . Will I ever go back there now?*

He stood out in the watering hole, the water lapping around

his waist, and looked up at Mud. What was supposed to happen now? He couldn't feel anything. . . .

"Do you accept me as your Great Father?" he called out, turning, peering over the hippos' heads to look for a friendly face in the crowd. The silence that followed was painful, but at last, a lioness from Gallantpride stepped forward.

"I accept you as Great Father," she said.

Bramble gave her a grateful smile.

"I accept you as Great Father," echoed another voice, and Bramble turned in the water to see a zebra step to the edge of the watering hole and dip its head to him.

A huge buffalo stepped forward next, raised his head, and looked Bramble in the eye—and then he startled, rearing back, almost crushing the smaller animals that stood close to him.

"Snakes!" he bellowed. "Look out! Everyone, get back!"

Bramble spun in the water with a splash, and saw the thin shapes emerging from cracks in the rocks, from right below Mud's feet, even falling from the trees beside the watering hole and landing on the backs of the gathered animals. Screams and honks of fear rose into the air as the animals of Bravelands panicked, some of them stamping or snapping at the snakes, some turning tail and running away. The hippos turned, their huge bodies churning up the water around Bramble and almost knocking him off his feet. Bramble tried to look for Moonflower, or for Mud or Moth, but they were lost amid the chaos.

"Protect the Great Father!" commanded Gentle Breeze, and her hippos began to chomp and thrash. Bramble was buffeted and slammed against the flank of one of the hippos, and the rising panic of the creatures around him filled his heart. He was about to die—either killed by the snakes, finally meeting the same fate he'd been trying to avoid for so long, or trampled by the very animals that had sworn to protect him. . . .

He thought he heard Moonflower's voice, over the howling and bellowing. "No, let me go! I have to help!"

Through the churning water, Bramble could see his death swimming toward him, long bodies too slippery and nimble for the hippos to grasp them all. He reached out and slammed his fist down on one as it came closer, but the water cushioned the blow, and the snake didn't even stop moving, but tangled itself around his arm. He tried to shake it off, but slipped and crashed into the water as he felt something move beneath his feet. He felt his ankles pulling together under the pressure of something winding around his legs, dragging him under.

He flailed with his free arm but couldn't stop himself sinking below the surface. Everything below the water was quiet and green and horrible. Streams of bubbles hid almost everything from view, but he saw the enormous green snake that had wrapped around his ankles, and the smaller ones swimming toward him, freakishly nimble in the water.

He kicked with his bound legs and managed to reach the air again, gulping in a panicking breath. He saw the horrified face of Gentle Breeze as water splashed over his face. One of the other hippos turned and lunged for him, but Gentle Breeze put her enormous body between them.

"No, Distant Star! You'll crush him!"

Bramble's gasping breath was cut off as he felt a snake crawl up his back and over his neck, wrapping tight around it. He sank back underwater, grasping at his throat.

Great Spirit, help me! he begged. *Please, I don't want to die like this. . . .*

His vision pulsed along with his racing heart, black clouds gathering all around him, and something even worse swam into view—long, knobbled snout open, rows of sharp teeth bared, a crocodile was slipping through the water, coming right for his face. He writhed with all the strength he had left, trying to tug his neck away from the crocodile's waiting jaws, and the teeth snapped down on the snake that clung around his shoulders instead of burying themselves in his flesh. He let out a bubble of triumph and tried to tug away—but then the crocodile, instead of trying again to end his life, gave a great heave and ripped the head of the snake from its body. The tightening coils around Bramble's neck went limp. He shook them off and tried to push for the surface again. The crocodile swam around him, and he felt a rough shove from below his back as he was pushed up and out of the water.

"Bramble!"

Black hands grabbed under his arms, dragging him through the water.

"I've got you," Moonflower said. "Valor, help!"

Bramble felt himself shoved, dragged, and rolled into the shallows. He coughed up water as he felt the pressure around his ankles loosen, and he looked around to see one of the lionesses rearing back with half a snake dangling from her jaws.

Bramble flopped onto his back and lay in the mud, the breath rasping in his throat, birds wheeling dizzily above him. He looked into Moonflower's worried face.

"Guess this isn't how that was meant to go," he croaked.

It wasn't over. He could hear the sounds of splashing and stomping as the animals fought the snakes, and he tried to sit up, but his head spun.

"Wait, what's that in the—get back, it's a crocodile!" he heard Moth shout.

"Gentle Breeze," said Mud's voice, wavering with emotion. "Take out that sandtongue!"

"No, wait," Bramble tried to yell, but his voice came as barely a whisper. "Moon, help." He reached out to Moonflower, who let him grasp her arms and start to pull himself up.

"That's not any crocodile!" said another voice.

The frantic stamping and braying had died down a bit, and almost all the animals at the edge of the watering hole were scampering back in fear as the crocodile walked out of the water onto the muddy bank. But not Spider. The elderly baboon was running forward, arms outstretched.

"Chew!" he exclaimed, and threw his arms around the crocodile's long muzzle and hugged it tight. Then he pulled away. "What happened to the rest of your bask? How did you end up—oh, really?" He paused, his head tilted. The crocodile looked up at him, nodded its great head, and looked over his shoulder and then back at the baboon. "Oh!" said Spider.

"The Great *Mother*? Are you sure?"

Mud pushed his way through the watching animals, slipping between the legs of a giraffe, and hurried over to Spider with Moth scrambling at his heels.

"What is going on, Spider?" he asked. "Do you . . . know this sandtongue creature?"

"Pssht," said Spider. "Know him? This is Chew! But never mind about that now. Look!"

He pointed over Bramble's shoulder, into the sun. Mud looked up and gasped. Bramble followed Spider's pointing finger, scooting around in the mud of the bank. The sun was low in the sky, almost blinding to look at across the plains, and two creatures were running toward them, but only one of them cast a shadow—the other one, silhouetted against the sun, for a moment looked like a creature made entirely out of shadow.

Of course, it was Prance, and she wasn't made of shadow at all—as she drew closer, she was the same small gazelle she had always been, ordinary-looking except for the shadow she didn't cast. But as she approached, Bramble heard a slow intake of breath from Mud.

"Oh . . . ," he said.

"Stop the gathering!" Gallant called out, as the two of them ran up and stopped in front of Mud. "A mistake is being made here. Animals of Bravelands, hear me!" he roared, and his voice seemed to shake the trees around him. "Your next Great Parent stands beside me! Prance Herdless has felt the Great Spirit's presence within her—she can speak skytongue and sandtongue, and she can send her own spirit far from her physical body, just as Great Father Thorn could do!"

"Prance," said Mud, his voice sounding a little strangled. "Is this true?"

There was a great rustling, like a high wind in the trees on the mountain, and Bramble looked up to see the birds, which had been circling high above, beginning to descend. Vultures and nightjars and plovers and eagles and so many more, settling in the trees and on the ground around Prance, a few of the smallest even landing on her horns.

Bramble's breath caught at the sight, wonder tightening his throat for a moment, before he let out a long and heavy sigh of awe, reverence . . . and relief. Tension seeped from his shoulders and his hands rested in the cool mud as he gazed at the true, indisputable Great Parent.

Prance met his eyes, dipped her head, and gave a bashful smile.

CHAPTER NINE

Prance took a deep breath. Every animal gathered at the watering hole was looking at her. She felt an unaccountable urge to turn and run, deny it all, shake off the birds—after all, they couldn't talk to anyone *else*, so who was to say whether they could talk to her?

But she didn't really want that. And no matter what she wanted, she had a duty now.

"It's true," she said, dipping her head to Mud respectfully. She spoke in a low voice, just to him, trying to ignore the stares from the giraffes and lions and meerkats and everyone else. "I understand that it's a surprise. Great Father Thorn passed the Spirit on to me as he died, but I wasn't sure of what it meant. I thought it might just be that I was carrying the Spirit for now, like Sky did—but my feathered friends have made it clear that that's not true."

"They certainly have," said the old baboon, scratching his head. He stared at her for a moment, and then he bowed deeply, putting both his front paws on the ground, and spoke in a voice that carried farther than hers had, even though it was weak. "Please accept my apologies. I misunderstood the stones—no, that's not true. I made assumptions. I allowed my prejudices to get the better of me. But I accept you, Prance Herdless, as Great Mother."

"Thank you," said Prance softly. She cleared her throat and tried to match his formal tone, speaking up so that all the animals could hear as she made herself sound as confident and Great Parent-ish as she could. "I know you just want the best for Bravelands. I do too. I accept your apology, and your fealty. You have a good heart, Mud Starleaf. Great Father Thorn prized your advice, and I will do the same, if you'll help me. I'll need wise counselors on my side."

Mud looked up, winced a little and put a paw on his back, and then shakily straightened up. "I would be proud, Great Mother."

"We should have a ceremony," said Bramble. He got up from the muddy bank of the watering hole. He was drenched, splattered with earth, and there was still part of a snake hanging from his shoulder, which his sister brushed off quickly. "To anoint the true Great Parent. I renounce any claim I mistakenly thought I had to the title and accept you, Prance, as Great Mother."

Prance nodded at him, and he bowed. As he straightened

up again, she was pretty sure she saw a sparkle of relief in his dark eyes.

"The watering hole may be too dangerous," said Mud. "We tried to guard the Great—Bramble—as best we could, and the snakes still almost killed him." He cast a confused glance at Chew, and Spider patted the crocodile proudly on the back of the head. "Grandmother clearly wants to prevent us from anointing the next Great Parent."

"Um, Mud?" Moth stepped forward. She looked up at Prance and gave a quick bow herself—Prance could see her friend's utter delight on her face, and it made her heart warm. "Is there any reason the ceremony *must* take place in the water? Couldn't we just do it right here, under the trees?"

"She has a point," said a voice.

Prance startled. That voice . . . but it didn't make any sense. Thorn was dead, he couldn't be here. . . .

But there he was, walking between the animals. He moved easily, his fur thick and his eyes bright, with no sign of the age or confusion that had troubled him at the end of his life, and very little sign of the fact that he was dead, either. He stepped closer, pausing for a moment to look with fondness on Mud and Moth, and Prance realized there was a shimmer to his fur, a spectral, glistening quality.

Prance cast her eyes from side to side, just checking that she was the only one who could see this shimmering Great Father, but none of the other animals had reacted to him at all. Mud and Moth were still talking about where the anointing should take place, but their voices seemed dim and far away while she was looking at Thorn.

Not even the vultures who sat by the side of the watering hole, pecking at the bodies of the snakes, seemed to see the Great Father as he passed them by.

"The watering hole is an old tradition. Perhaps one you can resurrect, when your time comes to join us—if you choose. But we can do this anywhere," Thorn said. "Moth's right, those trees look like the perfect place to me."

Prance turned to look at the trees where most of her bird escort were perched, and she caught her breath.

Other shimmering creatures were standing there beneath the trees, forming an open circle. Several elephants, a rhino, a cheetah, two leopards, a buffalo . . . they were all watching her and Thorn with friendly, ghostly interest. An enormous elephant blinked happily and gestured to Prance to come toward them.

She faintly heard the confused calls of the living animals behind her as she approached the trees. Bramble's voice, Valor's, Moth's . . . they were part of another world right now. The Great Parents of the past stood back to let her pass into the center of their ring, and she turned around, gasping, as the wind began to pick up all around her. The birds took flight from the trees as their branches began to shake and sway back and forth.

She tried to look into the faces of the Great Parents, but there were too many—somehow, though they made a circle no wider than the trees, there seemed to be an infinite number of faces gathered around her. There were elephants there beyond counting, their silver hides glistening, but among them there was a lioness, a turtle, an ibis, and even a great green snake. There were predators and herd animals, grasstongues and skytongues and sandtongues. Prance's breath caught as she looked into the glittering black eyes of a tall, elegant gazelle.

"The Great Spirit moves among us," said Mud's voice, a long way away. Prance tore her gaze from the other gazelle's face to turn and focus on the living animals once more. They were following her, forming a wider circle outside the ring of Great Parents. Mud, Moth, and Spider stood close to Thorn, though they didn't know it.

The grass blew around her hooves as if a great wind was blowing directly upon her, and when she looked up she saw that the birds were flying around the trees, dipping and weaving, but ever circling, like one huge and varied flock.

The living animals dipped their heads, and the Great Parents followed suit. Prance felt a great rush of air fill her lungs and reared up on her hind legs, throwing her horns back and closing her eyes as the power of the Great Spirit almost seemed to lift her up from the ground.

When her hooves struck back down in the grass, all at once, the wind was gone. She opened her eyes slowly, panting with exhilaration, and saw that the Great Parents were gone. The grass was still, the swaying of the trees coming to a gentle stop.

"Look to the mountain, Great Mother," said Thorn's voice, and she looked down to see him still there, though his shimmering fur was fading, melting away into mist, and then nothing. "And good luck."

There was a long moment of silence. Then Moth let out a whoop of triumph, drumming her fists on the ground.

"Great Mother Prance!" she cried. "All hail Great Mother Prance!"

"Hail, Great Mother!" the other animals took up the cry, and Prance turned on the spot, nodding and smiling—though she didn't feel quite as jubilant as she might have. Thorn's last words lay heavily on her back.

"Mud," she said, trotting up to him. "I received a . . . a message. I have to go. Gallant can guard me while I'm gone, but I have to go now. I'll be back as soon as I can."

She didn't wait for him to answer. She sat down in the grass, tucking her hooves beneath her chest, and closed her eyes.

When she opened them again and stood up out of her body, she saw Moth putting a hand on Mud's shoulder and pointing at Prance's shadow-self.

Mud squinted at the spot where Prance was standing, as if he could half see her, but wasn't quite sure of it.

Prance turned tail and bolted out from the trees, out across the plains, moving at the speed of shadow toward the mountain. She ascended into the air, and little puffs of cloud formed where her hooves struck.

At the very top of the mountain, she could see smoke rising, growing thicker, darker by the moment. But something else was happening, too. The lower slopes of the mountain seemed to shiver. The trees were moving, almost like they just had for her, the dense leaves of the jungle trembling.

Another earthquake? she thought. But it wasn't an earthquake. She began to catch glimpses of black fur, at first just a few, then more and more. Gorillas—*hundreds* of gorillas—marched out from the jungle, striking the ground with their knuckles as if they could pound the very earth into submission. Their eyes were fixed ahead, on the plains. They didn't slow or stop, and they didn't look around or pause for breath.

Prance turned tail and fled back to her body, struggling to shake the feeling that the gorillas were right behind her all the way.

"Grandmother's army," she said, before she'd even opened her eyes. She blinked and looked up at Mud, Moth, Bramble and Moonflower and Gallant, who had all gathered around her. They looked startled to see her spring to her hooves once more. "The gorillas are on the move. There are hundreds of them. They will be on the plains before the sun sets. We must do something."

"Hundreds?" gasped Bramble. "Are you sure?"

Prance nodded. "It was quite a sight. At least twice as many gorillas as there are gazelles in Runningherd, all of them walking with one purpose. And each of them as big and strong as either of you. Many of them much bigger."

"Father," whispered Moonflower, sadly.

"It sounds like him," said Bramble. "Our father, Burbark, was bitten by the snakes. He serves Grandmother now. But you would never usually see so many gorillas working together! Our troop was big, but it was still only a few families."

"Grandmother's influence must be spreading," said

Moonflower darkly. "I'm glad we're not there to fall under her spell too."

"The Spirit Mouth prophecy is coming true," Bramble said. "Evil is spreading from the mountain."

"And we must stand in its path, together," Prance said. She felt a steady confidence in her heart that she had almost never felt in her life before, even when she'd had the Us to guide her. The Great Spirit was her Us now, and all of Bravelands was her herd. Even so, she also felt the raging river of panic running underneath everything, ready to burst through at any moment. "But the gorillas are so strong. I don't know how we're going to stop them."

"I'll go," said Bramble. "I'll go and meet them."

"And what are you going to do when you get there?" asked Gallant.

"Talk to them," said Bramble firmly. "We're still gorillas, after all. Perhaps I can reason with them. I know they don't want to do this. Gorillas are peaceful creatures! We left the plains because we hated the bloodshed we saw here. There must be a way I can remind them of that."

Prance shifted her hooves uneasily. "It's just because you're gorillas that we need you and Moonflower on our side," she said. "I don't want to lose you. But if you think there's a chance you can prevent a fight, then we have to try."

"I'll go with you," said Mud. "I may be old and sometimes foolish, but I've stood beside Thorn as he's negotiated a truce between warring creatures more times than I can count. I will do everything I can to help you get through to them. And we won't go by ourselves—I'll choose a large troop of the strongest baboons to go with us."

Bramble nodded.

Prance stepped up to him and laid her forehead carefully against his shoulder.

"Good luck. Come back alive," she said. "Don't risk anything you can't afford to lose. That's an order from your new Great Mother."

"Yes, Great Mother," said Bramble with a smile.

Prance stepped back and watched as Bramble and Mud turned and started to walk away.

I've only been Great Mother for less than a day, she thought. *And already, I feel like I'm making decisions my friends might regret. . . .*

CHAPTER TEN

Chase took a deep sniff of wonderful, fresh air. Her aching paws padded a little faster as she climbed through the tunnel, as the cracks in the ceiling grew wider and came more frequently. All at once, she was walking under the blue sky, and the tunnel was now the bottom of a deep and twisting ravine. She paused to feel the breeze stirring her fur.

The urge to make a run for it rose once again in her heart, but, regretfully, she pushed it down. Grandmother showed no sign of wanting to kill her right now, but trying to get away would still be fatal. And there must be something she could do or say or learn, alone with Grandmother, that would help stop her. She had come this far: it would serve nobody if she got herself killed now, for the sake of a few moments of freedom.

She couldn't help thinking of Shadow and Seek, wondering

again where they were, what they thought had happened to her. The idea twisted in her stomach like a worm in a bird's beak, and she tried to turn away from it.

The ravine that had been the tunnel kept sloping upward, the cliff sides growing less steep and less high, until finally the rocks opened up before her, and Chase found herself walking out onto a scrubby, craggy mountainside. She could see the slopes rolling into the distance, undulating down to the plains. The view was incredible, and unsettling: instead of the green and shady jungle on the mountain she knew, here there was almost no shade, and very little except hardy yellow grass and spiky ferns grew between the stones. She blinked in the sunlight, tasting the air again and staring down at the plains as they rolled out ahead of her, with nothing standing between her and them but rock and open air.

Look behind you, said Grandmother's voice in her head. Chase paused to steel herself and then turned.

There was the ravine she'd just climbed up through, and there was the slinking, enormous shape of Grandmother herself. But it wasn't the giant snake that caught her eye. From here, she could see the green mountain slopes that they'd left far behind—and there was something wrong with them. Smoke belched from the high peak where they had entered the tunnels—not steam now, but unmistakably smoke, thicker and blacker, like the smoke Chase had seen once when a lightning strike had set some trees ablaze when she was just a cub.

"It's burning!" she gasped. "What happened?"

The smoke is a child of the fire snake, said Grandmother. She slithered up out of the ravine and circled Chase—not squeez-ing, not even touching, but before she could react Chase was completely surrounded by Grandmother's glistening scales. Grandmother raised her head to tower over Chase, over all the rocks nearby, and stared back at the mountain. *The smoke climbs into the sky to do battle with the skytongue. Nothing on land or in the air will be safe from the fire snake's coils, when the time comes.*

Chase shuddered.

If it wasn't safe to be on the mountain . . . that meant Shadow and Seek were in danger after all, no matter what sacrifices she'd made. She hoped, with every hair on her pelt, that they had the sense to get away from there even though she was missing. . . .

Now, be silent, Grandmother said, suddenly dipping her head again to the ground, moving faster than anything so large should be able to. Her tongue flickered out, tasting the air. *This place is full of enemies. Follow me, and be careful.*

Grandmother slithered around the rocks, hiding herself in the long shadows across the jagged landscape. Chase fol-lowed, choosing a path that was less obscured, where she knew she could stand on solid ground. She knew how to be quiet—she had stalked prey through the dripping jungle all her life, she knew how to place her paws so that she dis-turbed none of the loose rocks that gathered in all the cracks between the larger boulders.

But she didn't see any enemies lurking around the moun-taintop or between the rocks. What was Grandmother trying to avoid? Was there something she was afraid of?

There was no river or stream that Chase could see, but there were wide, shallow pools of water dotting the ground. A fine layer of steam rose from each one. Chase slunk between two of the pools and patted at the surface of the water, drawing her paw back quickly as she realized the pools were strangely warm.

Quiet! They're here, said Grandmother. Chase shook off her paw and padded silently along Grandmother's huge body to her head. She was peering through a gap between two tall rocks. Chase's ears flattened as she looked over the snake's head and saw that on the other side there was another wide, shallow pool, surrounded by tall, arching stones, and the space around the pool was full of vultures. They perched on the rocks, pecked at the water, preened under their large gray-brown wings.

These were Grandmother's enemies?

Stay here, said Grandmother, and she pressed on, slithering around the circle of rocks, her tongue flickering out and tasting the air.

What was she going to do?

Chase crouched at the gap and watched, her heart in her throat. The vultures seemed not to sense either of them. A young one splashed in the warm pool, shaking the water from his feathers, and a droplet fell on Chase's nose, but she didn't even dare to flinch.

Grandmother's scales moved so slowly, she could almost be mistaken for a pile of rocks—but at last, her nose appeared in between the stones, her jaw beginning to open, and still none of the vultures had seen it. . . . If Chase called out to warn them, Grandmother would kill her, but she couldn't just stand here and watch her swallow them whole. . . .

Tensing every muscle in her body, Chase shifted a paw and kicked at one of the small stones underneath her.

The vultures tensed. They looked up. They saw Grandmother's open maw swooping down on them. They tried to fly away. In seconds, chaos filled the space between the stones. Feathers flew, and water splashed, the vultures screamed, and Grandmother let out a furious hiss.

Chase's heart thumped in her chest, triumph and horror fighting inside her like angry cubs.

Some of the vultures had taken to the air, flapping madly, and were circling high above where even Grandmother's huge mass couldn't reach them. But others weren't so lucky. Grandmother snapped at one of the birds and caught it as it tried to lift off from the ground, and with a single horrid toss of her head she swallowed it down. Another vulture tried to take off, but its thinning wings weren't strong enough, its tailfeathers sodden and dragging it down. Grandmother watched it struggle for what seemed like a cruelly long time, following its movements with the swaying of her giant head. Younger, faster vultures kept darting down, as if they were trying to help their trapped elder, but they couldn't get close to Grandmother. . . .

Then, just as it looked like the old vulture might escape the pool, Grandmother snapped out and caught it on its wing, slamming it back down into the pool with a splash. It lay there, twitching, one wing clearly broken.

The circling vultures screamed and dived.

Chase's breath caught, her ears pinned back to her head, as the vultures poured down on Grandmother, sharp claws and beaks scratching and pecking. They struck off her scales almost as if they were made of stone, and she swung her huge body from side to side, catching one in her jaws, smashing another against the rocks. Grandmother's furious hissing echoed across the mountainside, and then suddenly she let out a different noise, a sort of sharp screech. Chase saw that somehow, in all the chaos, the old vulture that had landed helplessly in the pool had managed to get up after all, its wing not broken enough to stop it from fluttering up onto the top of Grandmother's head. It was clinging on with its claws, plunging its beak into Grandmother's eye. Black blood dribbled down the snake's cheek.

Chase was frozen, watching all this, until suddenly she heard a hoarse cry from behind her, and she looked up just in time to duck and shield her own eyes. Vultures had found her. She felt their claws tighten in her fur and leaped to her paws, growling, trying to shake them off.

I'm on your side! she wanted to scream, but she couldn't even catch her breath, suddenly mobbed by raging birds. She squeezed her eyes closed, tossed her head, and snapped her jaws, staggering backward. Her rear paws splashed into warm water, and she yelped and charged forward, trying to find a hole or a gap in the rocks that she could crawl into until it was over, one way or another ... but blinded by feathers and panic, she tried to spring over a rock, and her front paws came down on nothing. Her stomach turned over as she fell into empty air, and then her paws struck stone, and she rolled and tried to catch herself, but the rocks came up to meet her, striking her on the side of the head.

Chase lay still, her sides heaving. The sky was turning black, spinning around her, like the circling wings of the vultures. . . .

She squeezed her eyes shut again and took a breath, and then another, expecting to be raked by beaks and claws . . . but there were none. Her eyelids fluttered open, and she looked up at the sky. It was blue and empty. No vultures, only clouds, far above, moving fast.

She rolled over and staggered to her paws, looking around. The shadows were different—it wasn't sunset yet, but the sun had definitely moved. She must have passed out. How long had she been lying there?

She looked up and saw the ledge she had fallen from, and then she looked down, and regretted it—a dizzying drop stretched away, not more than a few paws-width from where she'd come to rest.

It was quiet, too. The only sign of the chaos was the occasional feathers that fluttered on the rocks.

Slowly, awkwardly, on bruised paws, she clambered back up the slope she had fallen down, pulling herself up over the ledge, and looking toward the circle of stones where the vultures had fought Grandmother. There was the unmistakable red-and-black bulk of Grandmother's tail. It wasn't moving.

Chase's heart began to pound, the aches in her paws and her head throbbing. Could it really be over?

Then the tail twitched, and once again she heard Grandmother's voice in her head.

Lie down and die, Windrider, she said. *The time of the vultures is over!*

Chase raised a paw to step closer and almost put it down right on the wing of a fallen vulture.

Reluctantly, she approached the stones. She padded between them and gasped.

Grandmother was there, her head reared up, looming over the pool, and all around her lay dozens of dead vultures. Grandmother's scales, which had seemed almost invincible, were scratched and damaged, a few of them even torn out. The eye that the old vulture had pecked was squeezed shut, still oozing black fluid. The vultures had done what no other creature had ever managed, what Chase had not even dared to try: they had hurt Grandmother, and badly.

But they had paid a terrible, terrible price.

In the middle of the pool, surrounded by the corpses of vultures, feathers sodden with water and with the blood of its kind, the elderly vulture that Grandmother had captured was still alive, despite it all. It looked up at Grandmother, its head swaying weakly.

Grandmother stiffened, and her head snapped around to focus on Chase with her one good eye.

Ah. Chase. Grandmother's voice in her mind was low and angry. It felt like it reached inside her chest and rattled her rib cage. *Come here. Dispatch this upstart vulture for me. Kill her, and show her that all of Bravelands will soon be mine.*

Chase hesitated.

"She's almost dead," she whispered, without thinking. "This isn't a hunt. The—the Code . . ."

The Code?! Grandmother swung around, coming face-to-face with Chase in a single smooth, sudden movement. *Are you my protector or not? You failed me today. You ran. The Code means nothing! It is something weak animals invented to control the strong!* She seemed to take a deep breath, and Chase thought she saw her wince. *You're welcome to join Range if you cannot do your duty,* she hissed in Chase's mind. *Do you refuse?*

Maybe I can't do this, Chase thought. *Maybe it would be better to join Range in her stomach than stay here and murder this helpless vulture for her. . . .*

Chase's gaze drifted to the vulture herself. She was hunched, pathetic, turning her head to look up at Chase. . . .

Chase Born of Prowl, came a voice—but this wasn't Grandmother. The voice was softer, kinder, underlined with a harsh echo like the distant caw of a bird. *Do as you're told. For the good of Bravelands. My time has come.*

The vulture blinked at her.

I have foreseen my death, it said. *Strike me down now, and live to save your family, and all of Bravelands. I have spoken. It must be.*

For a second, Chase still wasn't sure that she could. But then, at last, she nodded slowly.

"No, I don't refuse," Chase yowled. "Sorry, Grandmother."

Then tear this vulture's head off and be done with it, Grandmother said, withdrawing as quickly as she'd advanced, leaving Chase a clear path to the pool.

Chase padded over, pushing aside all her hesitation. The least she could do, for this strange old wise creature, was make its death quick.

The vulture looked up at her as she raised her paw, claws extended.

This is a good death, the vulture said.

Chase brought down her paw.

CHAPTER ELEVEN

Bramble's fists were stiff and scuffed from the long walk across the hard earth of the plains. The sun was slipping closer and closer to the horizon, as Bramble, Moonflower, Mud, and their troop of baboons walked in and out of the long shadow of trees. He knew they made a strange sight, the two gorillas knuckling ahead, towering over their baboon companions. They didn't talk. They stopped only once, to drink from a stream while they still could.

How far would they have to go before they met the gorillas coming the other way? How quickly would Grandmother's marching gorilla army move?

Bramble squinted into the distance, searching the wavering grass for the black-and-silver bodies of his family, but he didn't see them between the trees, or across the ravine. . . .

He was starting to wonder if, somehow, Prance could have

been wrong. *Great Mother* Prance, that was.

It was a bigger relief than he wanted to admit, *not* being the Great Parent. He still wanted to help Bravelands. He would do what he could to stop Burbark. But it had felt like a weight the size of the mountain had been lifted from his shoulders, the moment he'd realized that Prance was everything he'd been telling himself he had to be.

The ground underfoot was rising now, not into the foothills of the mountain yet, but up to a hill that Bramble thought was the edge of a ravine, maybe a riverbed. There were a few wide, spreading acacia trees long the top of the small hill, and Bramble headed toward them, planning to stop in their shade and see if they'd found a vantage point to spot the gorillas on the horizon.

He climbed up the hill, and when he got to the top, he had to put out a hand to steady himself against the trunk of the tree. The gorillas weren't on the horizon—they were right in front of him. The hill sloped down to the muddy bed of a shallow river, and on the other side were dozens and dozens of gorillas, knuckling across the plains, the foggy foothills of the mountain vanishing in the distance.

Moonflower came up the hill behind him, and he heard her soft intake of breath as she cast her eyes on the approaching gorillas.

They were moving wrong. He couldn't put his finger on why, exactly—if he watched one of them at a time, they looked like they were walking normally. But as they reached the river, they all slowed at the same rate, all stopped the same distance from the shallow water. As if one mind was controlling a hundred gorillas, all at once . . .

"We've picked up an audience," Moonflower muttered, looking over her shoulder. Bramble glanced back and saw that as well as the baboons who were gathering around and staring down at the massive troop with jaws hanging open and worried eyes, a small herd of animals were following them curiously—zebras, a lone prowling hyena, a troop of chattering meerkats, and some others.

"This is wrong," said Mud, leaning on the tree trunk, shaking his head. "I believed the Great Mother, but . . . this is so wrong. . . ."

There were animals gathering on the other side of the river too, flocks of birds and a few scattered gazelles, watching the gorillas with amazement.

They couldn't know how bad this is. Gorillas are strangers in these parts. And we're peaceful grass-eaters.

No creature who hadn't seen two silverbacks clashing, or a Goldback defending her baby from predators, could know just how much danger they might be in right now.

Moonflower grabbed Bramble's shoulder. "There he is," she said.

Bramble looked down and found his eyes drawn to a shambling black-and-silver body making its way to the edge of the river.

Burbark Silverback looked up at Bramble and Moonflower, and they stared back at their father. He looked . . . different. The silver hair on his back was thinner and duller. His back and arms, once broad and bulging with muscles, looked diminished.

"What happened to him?" Moonflower breathed.

"The venom," Bramble said. "He's the one who's been under the sandtongue curse the longest. This is what Grandmother's poison is doing to him."

He took a deep breath and knuckled forward, out of the shadow of the trees, so he was standing alone on the steep bank down to the river. He took a deep breath, swelling his chest.

"Burbark Silverback," he called out. "Do you remember your son, Bramble? I've come to talk!"

A murmur of gossipy excitement went up from the band of meerkats farther along the bank. A few more animals had gathered behind them.

Burbark didn't respond aloud, but he stepped forward into the shallow and muddy water, leaving the ranks of other gorillas standing on the bank staring ahead, swaying a little. Bramble suddenly wondered how long they'd been marching down from the mountain, how tired they must be—or would be, if they could even feel their own feelings anymore with Grandmother's curse living in their minds.

There was movement in the water around Burbark's feet. Two long crocodiles swam up from the muddy bed to flank him as he moved toward the middle.

"I don't suppose those are more of Spider's crocodiles?" asked one of the baboons.

"Maybe they were, once," said Bramble darkly, and began

to walk down the bank toward his father.

Moonflower was right behind him, but Bramble's skin prickled as he felt the gazes of all the gathered animals on him, uncomfortably similar to the stares of the animals as he'd waded into the watering hole to become the new Great Father.

Very similar. I still don't know what in the name of the Great Spirit I'm trying to do.

Close up, Burbark's wasting was even more pronounced. His jowls hung loose around his face, and his movements were tense and jittery. It was tragic to see him like this, but somehow, he was no less frightening.

"Father," Bramble said. "Gorillas do not live on the plains. What are you doing here?"

"*Father*'?" Burbark echoed as he tilted his head and stared into Bramble's eyes. Bramble shuddered. There was no recognition there. "We are no fathers. We are no sons," Burbark intoned as he raised an arm and turned to the watching animals. Bramble remembered the days when a roar from him would send all the birds of the forest flying from the trees. "We are more than mere gorillas. We are the fingers, and the hands. We reach. We grasp. We tear. We are Her instruments in this world."

Moonflower was standing beside Bramble now, her toes in the water, and he suddenly realized she was shaking, but not with fear.

"What has she done to you? To all of you?" Her hands clenched into fists. "You've lost your mind, and I know who's responsible. So where is she? Too afraid to come out and face us?"

Bramble gave his sister a look of alarm. *By the Great Spirit, be careful, Moonflower!*

Moonflower turned just as Burbark had and held up her arms.

"This is the work of the snake who calls herself Grandmother," she declared. "She has stolen their minds and made them into her claws!" She turned back to Burbark but kept her voice high and clear for everyone to hear. "I love my father, and I will tear her scales off for what she's done to him!"

Burbark didn't scream. He didn't lunge for her. He simply turned his head, just slightly, toward the assembled gorillas behind him. He raised one palm.

"Kill them," he said.

One of the crocodiles lunged, opening its jaw so wide Bramble could see right down its throat. Bramble leaped clear, dragging Moonflower with him. With a great lurch, the gorillas began to move. The first line of them stomped down the bank and into the river, churning it to mud with their fists.

"Too many of them," Bramble gasped. "Run."

Moonflower gave a shaky growl of rage and frustration and tugged against his grip for a moment. She slammed her fist down on the side of the crocodile's open jaw, sending a tooth flying into the water. But then she let him pull her away, and they both turned and scrambled for the trees. Something whistled over Bramble's head, and he looked up to see the baboons were gathered along the top of the slope or in the tree branches, gripping rocks and nuts and handfuls of dry earth. They started to pelt the gorillas and the crocodiles, and Bramble heard grunts and stumbling feet as their pursuers slowed under the rain of stones.

They made it to the top of the hill. Bramble spun around and saw the crowd of gorillas coming up behind him, some of them stopping to pick up the stones and hurl them back at the baboons. One hit the tree by Moonflower's shoulder and sent splinters flying into the air.

"Get down," she called up to the baboons in the tree. "We have to go!"

The baboons leaped down, and Moonflower scooped up Mud and threw him onto her back. They all began to back away, but one of the baboons was too slow, and Bramble watched in horror as a Goldback he used to know swung up into the tree and grabbed the baboon by the leg, tossing her down into the mass of marching gorillas. The baboon screamed, there was a wave of flailing fists, and she abruptly stopped screaming.

"Run," Moonflower said. "Bramble, *run!*"

Bramble paused one moment more, looking up the slope now, into the twitching face of Burbark as he was silhouetted below the acacia trees.

He choked back a cry of despair and guilt. He had failed.

Then he turned and, with Moonflower and the remaining baboons around him, ran for his life.

CHAPTER TWELVE

The sun had sunk beneath the horizon and the sky was glittering with stars. Prance was exhausted. So many of the animals had had questions for her. So many of them she'd been unable to answer. It was intimidating, and exhilarating, to be addressed as the Great Mother all day long—but whenever she felt a pang of doubt or worry, she closed her eyes, concentrated on the feeling of Thorn's paw over her heart, and asked the Great Spirit, and all the Great Parents before her, to be with her. Perhaps the warmth she felt in return was real, or perhaps it was only a memory, but it was comforting all the same.

She was grateful for Moth, who'd stepped into Mud's role without blinking, organizing and occasionally shooing away animals who wanted her attention. Now, as the initial rush of questions and concerns was ebbing away, Moth walked up to Prance with Gallant and a lioness following behind her. It was Valor—Gallant's mate, and the mother of the cub who was calling himself Terror. There was a look in her eyes of clouded, barely controlled desperation. It couldn't have been more than a few days since Gallant had told her that their cub was alive, and living with Menacepride. . . .

"Gallant and Valor would like a word," said Moth, dropping the formality that she'd adopted in front of most of the other creatures. "I thought you'd want to hear them out now."

Prance simply nodded.

"Great Mother," said Gallant. He nodded his large maned head and then leaned his shoulder against Valor. "Please, will you check again on . . . our cub?"

Were you going to say Valorcub, Prance wondered, *or were you going to call him Terror? Either must feel very wrong. . . .*

"Of course I will," she said. "Sit down with me, I'll be back as soon as I can."

She closed her eyes and unfolded herself, lurching to her shadow-legs, tossing her shadow-horns in the still air. The stars above her seemed brighter, and yet strangely seemed to shimmer less, almost as if she could see them more clearly in this form.

Making the transition seemed more natural every time— but she felt the exhaustion not only in her physical body, but in her shadow-self. It was a little harder to get moving, to spring into the air and rise over the plains.

My gift is not the gift of infinite movement, she thought, for the first time. *I can go very fast, and very far, but eventually I will have to rest. . . .*

Could she be too tired to get back into her body? She didn't want to find out. She knew where she had last seen Menace-pride, and she headed straight there, not slowing down to look around at the rest of Bravelands.

Sure enough, the pride were still nearby where they'd been before, lounging beside a lazy shallow river. But something was different . . . something was wrong . . .

She skittered to an anxious halt atop a nearby boulder, looking down at the pride, shuddering as she saw the snakes slithering between the lions. One of the elderly lionesses stirred and put her paw down on a snake that was making its way past her muzzle—but she didn't bite or claw it. She licked its scaly head, as if it was her cub, and then rolled over and went back to sleep.

I'm too late, Prance thought. She ran in a circle around the pride, searching for Terror, jinking with alarm as she saw the snakebites on the paws and tails of the lions. . . .

But Terror wasn't there. And neither was Menace.

Did they escape? Or were they killed? Or are they simply gone, hunting for prey for their cursed pride?

She turned on the spot, searching the horizon, but there was no sign of the cub or the elderly pride leader. One of the scarred male lions sat up and stretched, dislodging a snake that had been draped over his shoulders.

"We see you there, little shadow," he growled. Prance startled and backed away. "Our empress is coming closer, ever closer. She will eat the heart of Bravelands."

Behind him the other lions were stirring, one of the

lionesses crouching low to stalk Prance's shadow-form. Prance let out a squeak of fright and took off in a clumsy skitter of hooves, like a foal running from a hidden crocodile at the watering hole. The lions and their snake companions stared after her, unblinking, as she jinked and galloped her way across the night sky.

She slipped back into her body with a heavy sigh of relief and kept her eyes squeezed closed for a moment, breathing in the scent of the real grass under her folded legs, waiting for her rattled heartbeat to slow down. Then she opened her eyes and looked at Gallant and Valor, whose faces were twisted in obvious concern.

"What's wrong?" Valor asked as soon as Prance looked up. "What happened? Did something happen to my cub?"

Prance tried to take a long, considered breath before answering.

"I didn't see him," she said. "I found the other lions, but T—your cub and Menace were both missing. The other lions of Menacepride . . . they must have been too old, too slow. They were all bitten. They've been taken by the sandtongue curse."

Valor let out a pained roar and buried her head under her paws.

"But . . . but was . . . ," Gallant started, and then shook his mane. "Thank you, Great Mother."

"There's still hope," Prance said, wincing. "He and Menace might have gotten away—he was the youngest, and Menace . . ."

"Nothing will ever kill that moldy old lion," snarled Valor under her breath. "If a snake did bite her, the snake would be the one who got poisoned." She looked up at Gallant and pressed her forehead to his cheek. "There's hope. That's more than we've had for a long time."

"You should go," Prance blurted out. "Both of you should go out there and try to find him, if you need to."

Gallant and Valor looked at each other, and both took a deep breath. Something passed between them, and Prance wasn't sure what it was, but she felt almost as if she should look away.

"I promised Thorn that my pride would protect you," said Gallant, turning back to Prance.

"And we intend to keep that promise," added Valor. "We'll search for him, but we won't leave you undefended. That would be just what Grandmother wanted."

Prance nodded, almost lost for words. "Thank you," was all she could think to say.

Just as Gallant was turning away, Prance heard a shriek. Startled, she sprang to her hooves, turning in a clumsy circle in search of the source of the sound.

"Great Mother?" said Valor. "What's wrong?"

"What's making that noise?" Prance looked to the sky, wondering if it was a bird's cry, or if something somewhere was in terrible pain—the sound went on for a long couple of heartbeats and then trailed off.

"What noise?" Gallant asked.

Prance looked at him, saw he was serious, and then turned

her eyes to the sky once more. "There was a scream. It must have been a bird, or a sandtongue. . . ."

She began to walk, tripping over a tree root as she kept her eyes on the distant stars, trying to make her way in the direction the sound had come from. Gallant, Moth, and Valor fell in step behind her, even though they didn't hear the noise, and she was grateful for their company as she hurried out into the plain beyond the watering hole.

Then suddenly, a patch of stars above her winked and went out, and a moment later the darkness resolved into flying shapes: black vultures, wheeling out of the night and dropping into the grass in front of her. Prance ran over to them but skidded to a halt as she realized that they weren't real vultures.

"Shadows," she gasped.

There were dozens of them. They moved like vultures, but they were void and insubstantial, and the grass didn't move where they landed. None of them had eyes that she could see, but her skin prickled with the sense that they were all staring at her. They opened their shadow-beaks and let out another cry of pain and fear and grief that sent Prance staggering backward, almost stepping on Moth.

Then one more vulture landed in front of them, staggered a few steps forward, and collapsed. This one was real. Her feathers were ruffled and stained with rusty red, and she looked exhausted. Prance ran over and nuzzled her muzzle against her neck, praying to the Great Spirit that the vulture wasn't dying.

The bird looked up at her and tried to straighten up.

"Great Mother," said the vulture. She bowed her head, but then reeled as if the movement had made her dizzy.

"I'm here," said Prance. "It's all right. Take your time. What's your name?"

"Stormrider," said the vulture. She paused, catching her breath, ruffling her feathers.

"And what . . . what's happened to your flock?" Prance asked, after Stormrider had had a moment to gather herself.

Stormrider looked up, her beak slightly open. "How did you know?" she said. "We were attacked at the mountain pool. We tried to fight her off, but the great snake was just too strong. There was a leopard with her . . . and the whole flock . . . the whole flock is dead!"

Prance slowly looked up, over Stormrider's head. The flock of shadow-vultures regarded her with their blank, eyeless faces.

Then she let out a shaky breath and lowered her muzzle again to give Stormrider a very small, gentle lick on the top of her head.

"I'm so very sorry," she said.

"What's wrong?" whispered Moth. She and the two lions were both staring at Stormrider, obviously unable to see the mass of shadow-vultures just behind her.

"Grandmother is already here. She found her way to the vulture pool in the mountains. She had a leopard with her, and they attacked. All the other vultures are dead."

"No," said Moth, throwing her paws over her mouth. "But the vultures are—they're our link to the Great Spirit. They taste the deaths of Bravelands and help the Great Parent. They can't be gone!"

"Grandmother is attacking the very roots of the Great Spirit," Prance said. "She's trying to wither it out from underneath us. But she won't succeed."

CHAPTER THIRTEEN

Chase had hoped that being outside, with the wind in her fur and enough space to shake her tail, would feel good despite everything. And it *was* a relief not to be back in the tunnels, at least at first. She and Grandmother had descended from the mountain under the setting sun, and the light streaming through the clouds and the sight of Bravelands stretching out ahead of them was almost beautiful enough for Chase to forget about the vulture blood still drying on Grandmother's scales and on her own paws. For long moments at a time, she didn't think about the sound of the elderly vulture's voice in her head, or the heavy slithering of Grandmother behind her.

But the reality of it all always came back to her eventually. It settled on her shoulders until she almost felt like she was still walking through the tunnels, penned in on all sides by worry, and with only darkness ahead.

This is a good death, the vulture had said, and *Live to save your family, and all of Bravelands.*

But how could any of that be true? How could she make it come true, when Grandmother could choose, at any moment, to swallow her whole and move on as if she had never existed?

Night fell, and Chase kept trudging ahead, her head lolling, not bothering to ask the snake if they would stop—she knew she would be told, if it was time. Her paws ached, and her head had started to throb again after she'd hit it on the rocks up in the mountain. At last, when the sky had turned black and the stars were shining bright above them, they passed through a small forest, and Grandmother slithered to a halt in a clearing between tall fig trees.

We stop here, she announced. *The vultures took their toll on me. I must shed again. I am so close to my final, unstoppable form, I will not risk another conflict while I am still vulnerable.*

Chase stopped and nodded, looking around for the cave or tunnel where Grandmother would hide to shed her skin once more. But instead of slithering away, Grandmother curled her enormous body around and around in the clearing, then laid her head down.

We are out in the open, she said. *You will guard me while I am reborn. Nothing must interrupt the process, Chase. Do you understand?*

"Yes, Grandmother," said Chase. "I'll keep watch from the trees. Nothing will disturb you."

She forced herself to calmly leap up into the lower branches of the fig tree and laid down along a branch. She scented the air, as Grandmother's breathing slowed and became deeper. Was she asleep? It was impossible to tell—she had turned as still as a stone.

Chase could scent the trails of other creatures in the forest, but none that could be much help—small monkeys and rodents, and the nests of birds.

If only we could have run into some more leopards, she thought. *Or some rhinos, or even a pack of hyenas.*

But she was on her own, and she couldn't wait any longer. The fact lay heavy on her, like she'd swallowed a bunch of rocks. Grandmother had to be stopped, and she had presented Chase with the only opportunity she was ever going to get.

She leaped silently to the next tree branch and then the next, pretending to scout the surroundings, but really studying Grandmother from above. She could take her time—she had to wait for the shedding to begin. She positioned herself on a branch just behind where the snake's head lay. This was the side where the vultures had blinded her—if it wasn't fixed by shedding, it would give Chase a precious second's advantage. As soon as Grandmother pushed her head out, glistening and vulnerable, Chase would leap from here, dig her claws in, and there was the soft place behind the skull where she would sink her teeth. Something told Chase that Grandmother would be harder to kill than the prey she used to hunt up on the mountain, but she had to try.

Chase thought of her mother, Prowl, and of Shadow, and Seek's mother, and even of Range—the leopard that he might have been, if the sandtongue poison hadn't driven him mad before they ever even met.

She imagined they were all with her now.

Lend me your silent stalking, she prayed. *Lend me your strong jaws. I will not let go until one of us is dead. . . .*

Down below, there was a movement, and Chase tensed.

The shedding had begun, and it was the strangest thing that she had ever seen.

Without moving, or obviously changing very much at all in the starlit darkness, Grandmother had detached herself from her own skin. Chase could see her twitching, slowly wriggling, her scales moving, all within the pale sheath of her old skin. For a moment, she had two sets of scales, two sets of eyes, two mouths. The scars of the vulture attack that marred the old scales were nowhere to be found on the ones that moved underneath.

And then the jaws of the old skin began to peel away from Grandmother's lips, and the pale jaws opened, wider, wider, until Grandmother's glistening head was able to push through.

It was almost so distractingly horrible, to watch the giant snake emerge from its own jaws, that she wasn't ready to jump. She sucked in a deep breath, crouched back, shifting her weight back and forth, getting a fix on the spot on the back of Grandmother's head where she would place her claws. . . .

And then something smacked into her, out of the darkness. Then another something, and another. Furry hands and feet, tails and teeth latched on to her side as she scrambled and clawed to keep her grip on the tree branch, but her claws just tore the bark from the tree and then she was falling, clawing at nothing.

She thumped to the ground, landing on something soft. Grandmother's old tail. And three of the furry creatures were still on her, trying to pin her down. Vervet monkeys, their black faces ringed with a mane of pale gray hair—but these weren't just any monkeys. As she fought to stand up, more of them swarmed out of the trees, their eyes unfocused, snake-bites oozing on their necks and tails, smelling unmistakably of the venom in their veins. They grabbed her paws, her tail, they sat on her back and smacked her with their hard little fists when she tried to snap at them and shake them off.

Don't struggle, my dear, said Grandmother. Her enormous head came into view, one eye still shut but the other glinting in the starlight. *If I must have them tear your eyes from your head, I will.*

The monkeys' horrible questing fingers were pulling at Chase's ears and hooking into her cheeks. She stopped struggling.

Thank you, my loyal friends, said Grandmother, and the vervet monkeys let out a horrible chittering giggle, all at once. Trapped where she was, Chase could see a couple of them start to stroke and play with the shed skin, draping it over their heads and sniffing it as if it was a ripe, juicy mango.

I have sensed your disloyalty for some time, Chase, Grandmother admonished. *I knew that my gift wasn't quite the same for you as the gorillas. So I took precautions.*

Chase swallowed. She felt dizzy.

All that time, alone in the tunnels, with Grandmother's jaws literally on her tail, and she hadn't been safe, not for one pawstep.

If she thought she'd been afraid back then, it was nothing compared to the dawning horror that filled her now, as she thought of every moment she had considered running or fighting and told herself that it was better to wait, to keep Grandmother in the dark, for as long as possible.

But Grandmother knew. She had known the whole time. Death was waiting, right behind Chase, the whole time.

And then the vultures—had that been a test?

Chase swallowed again, tried to clear the fear out of her throat before she spoke. "Then why not just kill me?" she growled. "Why pick me to come here, alone with you?"

Your death serves no purpose, Grandmother said. *My gift is many things, but there are a few tasks that can be better completed with . . . let us say a sharper clarity of purpose.*

"What . . . tasks?" Chase snarled.

Tasks like the one you are about to do for me now, said Grandmother.

Chase closed her eyes. Even now, somehow, it wasn't over. Would it ever be over?

"I refuse," she said. She opened her eyes again and glared into Grandmother's one good eye. "Eat me, or have your monkeys tear me apart. I won't do another thing for you."

And once you are dead, Grandmother hissed, her long tongue flicking out to tickle Chase's ear, *would you like me to tell your dear mate, and the little cub, all about it? Before I have my gorillas grind their skulls into mud?*

"You're bluffing," Chase spat. "You don't know where they are."

Oh, I think I do. My gorillas captured them before we even left the mountain.

Chase's fur stood on end.

They have been walking, just as we have, but they are safe, Grandmother added. *For now. If you do this favor for me, you can all live, and run, and hope to be somewhere far away when the time of the sandtongue comes at last. If you refuse, you all die, and you will have failed to protect them, just as you failed to protect Prowl. It is quite simple.*

She still could have been bluffing. But Chase already knew she couldn't take that chance.

"What do you want me to do?"

Only what you are good at, said Grandmother. *Only what you were born to do. Hunt and kill.*

CHAPTER FOURTEEN

Bramble stumbled to a stop, his lungs burning and his knuckles and feet aching. The sound of the gorilla troop had faded behind them as the night had fallen, and as he looked back, he searched for any sign of Burbark or his army, but there was none. They'd outrun them.

The stars overhead seemed to pulse along with the beating of Bramble's heart, and he bent over, trying to catch his breath.

"I think we lost them," gasped Bug, one of the baboons, stumbling a few steps back and squinting into the dark.

"Should have brought more baboons," muttered another.

"Should have brought Gallantpride," said a third, "and the elephants, and maybe a herd of buffalo."

Bramble winced, staring at his hands, his head spinning.

"This is my fault," he said. "Mango's dead, and for nothing.

I brought you all this way. . . ."

"It's not your fault," said Moonflower sternly. She let Mud slip down from her shoulders and stretched out her arms. "This is Grandmother's fault, and no one else's, not even Bur-bark."

"I thought I could talk to him. I thought he'd listen to me." The words tumbled out of Bramble's mouth, like a confession to a secret, except it was a secret he hadn't realized he was keeping. *Why? Why did I think that? He tried to have us killed before we even left the mountain. I just forgot how completely he'd changed.*

I didn't want to remember.

"We can't sit here moping about it," muttered Bug.

Bramble looked up at Moonflower and found that she was staring into the distance, her hands loose at her sides, her eyes glazed. He peered into the darkness but couldn't see much on the horizon.

"What? What is it?" he asked.

Moonflower blinked.

"The smoke from the mountain," she said. "I saw something. I saw Prance. She was all alone, surrounded by shadows. . . . I think she's in danger."

She gave Bramble a frightened, lost look. Bramble found he didn't know what to say—Prance was almost certainly in danger. They all were. . . .

Then Moonflower looked down, and Bramble saw that Mud was holding her large hand in both his small ones.

"Then we must get back," he said. "We won't let anything happen to her."

"Yes, right," said Moonflower. She shook her head. "Yes, let's go."

They started off again, picking up the pace, Bug and two other baboons racing ahead to scout for predators that might be prowling in the night. The stars and the moon were bright, and the plains were active with the screeches of nocturnal creatures. Bramble remembered how scared he'd been, the first night he'd spent on the plains. It felt painfully ironic now that he was running from his own kind, the peace-loving gorillas of the mountain.

Bramble's knees were starting to become shaky, and he felt a shiver run down his spine.

He startled as three small shapes came running out of the dark toward them. It was the scouting baboons.

"Big herd of wildebeests up ahead," panted Bug. "They're blocking the passage through the ravine."

"Should we go around?" Moonflower asked.

"It'll be slower. Wildebeests are stubborn, but they won't bother us," said Mud. "Let's see if we can get through."

They walked on, the ground around them turning from open grassland to a rockier earth, where Bramble stubbed his toe more than once in the dim light. He remembered when they'd passed this way before: the ravine was wide, and at its deepest the cliff walls were ten gorillas high, at least, with twisting trees and vines growing right out of the packed earth.

The stars were going out, the sky beginning to take on the faint gray of the hours before dawn, when they came upon the huge mass of brown bodies that clogged the way into the ravine.

"Let us through," Mud announced, holding his paws up. "We're on urgent business for the Great Mother!"

Bramble tried to catch the eye of one of the wildebeests. He was thinking of the old wildebeest he and Moonflower had met on their way to the Great Father, the one who had accepted his death with such grace and good humor. . . .

The wildebeests snorted and shuffled their hooves. None of them replied to Mud, but eventually, with a sort of collective sigh of annoyance, they began to jostle each other and step aside.

"Thank you," Bramble said, and made for the gap that had opened up. It wasn't a huge gap—the gorillas and baboons had to walk single file through it, and a couple of times Bramble felt that the wildebeests might be thinking they were leaving room for something more baboon-size than gorilla-size. He stumbled, apologized to the wildebeest whose haunches he'd bumped his shoulders against, pressed on into the forest of brown hair. . . .

And then there was no more gap. He paused, one of the baboons walking into his back as he peered around.

"Excuse me," he said. "We need to get through, it's urgent!"

None of the wildebeests moved.

"Hey!" said Moonflower. "What are you doing?"

Bramble turned, but he couldn't see her—all he could see was a wall of brown bodies, cutting him off from the others.

He knuckled around in a circle, surrounded by wildebeests. One of them swung its head down to put its large black eye level with Bramble's face. It still didn't speak, but the way it was staring sent a terrible chill down Bramble's spine.

"We have to get out of here," he muttered.

"Where's your herd leader?" demanded Bug, her voice high-pitched with fear.

The wildebeests breathed, all of them together, and then the one whose eye was staring into Bramble's face spoke in a deep and raspy voice.

"We have a new leader now," he said. "Soon she will be here. Soon all creatures will sing her name."

The wildebeest took a step, and Bramble found himself squeezed between the flanks of two of the beasts. Another slammed into his shoulder, and one hoof trod on his foot— he thought in a panicked kind of daze that it must have been unintentional, because it hurt, but there was no crunching of bone. He heard yelps and shrieks as the others were squeezed too, wildebeest bodies crowding in around them. He managed to get one arm free and grabbed on to the nearest beast, trying to push it away, but he could move it only a little way before the mass of animals pressed back.

There was another angry screech, and Bramble craned his neck and saw Bug clamber up out of the press of wildebeests and onto one of the creatures' backs. She reached back and dragged another baboon after her, who reached for another. The wildebeests they were standing on roared and tossed their heads, but there wasn't room in the crush to throw them off once they'd flattened themselves to a wildebeest's back and grabbed on to its hair. All the baboons managed to squeeze and wriggle out of the crush, and then Mud leaned over, reaching for Bramble, and Bramble instinctively reached back. . . .

But then he pulled his hand away.

"I'm too heavy," he shouted. "Just go!"

"We can't—leave—*oof!*" Mud was tossed around and almost fell as the wildebeests reared up under him.

"Go!" Moonflower's voice rang out. "We'll be okay!"

Bramble saw a black-fingered hand pressing between the neck of one wildebeest and the flank of another, and he reached out and grabbed it. He put his shoulder into the creature's haunches and heaved, making just enough space that Moonflower managed to duck and wriggle through. The wildebeest roared and pushed back, sending them both staggering, but they held on to each other and just about stayed standing.

The baboons sprang for safety, running across the backs of the wildebeests and launching themselves at the vines that grew down the sides of the ravine.

We're going to die, Bramble thought, clinging desperately to Moonflower as the wildebeests screamed with rage and buffeted them from side to side, *but at least we'll be together.* . . .

A short, sharp horn jabbed through the air right toward his face, and he reeled back, grasping the horns in his fists to try to wrestle them out of the way. Moonflower yelped as another pair smacked her in the shoulder. Bramble saw red and tried to punch out at the wildebeest that had tried to gore him—but something was happening. The beasts behind his back were moving away; the whole herd was shifting. He let go of the horns to avoid being dragged, and another wildebeest ran right into him, sending him finally sprawling to the ground. Dust rose from the hooves of the herd and filled his eyes and his nose.

"They're trying to stampede—" Moonflower's voice was cut off in a gasp, as if she'd been winded.

Hooves trampled past and over Bramble, kicking him in the legs, in the ribs, as he threw his arms up to protect his head and tried to curl up, to make himself as small as he could. At last, he sensed a gap in the beasts and rolled to his feet just in time to see one hoofing the ground, horns lowered, preparing to charge.

"Bramble, look out!" Moonflower shrieked. He turned to see her clinging to a tree root that was growing out of the cliff wall, barely above the bucking horns of another wildebeest. Then he saw where she was pointing: another one, parted from the stampeding crowd, turning around to run back at Bramble.

Bramble dropped to the ground and threw himself head over heels out of the way, as the two wildebeests charged. He smacked into rocks at the cliff base and landed in a heap, just as there was a huge, terrible clacking and groaning from behind them. The two wildebeests had collided with each other, instead of spearing him through with their horns from both sides, and now they were stuck, or wrestling, or perhaps just confused—either way, Moonflower was climbing down and reaching for him, and Bramble wasn't going to stick around to watch. He leaped for her hand, gripped it, and hauled himself up onto the tree roots.

They both began to climb, followed all the way up the cliff by the furious honking and snorting of the wildebeest herd. It was a hard scramble, with crumbling rocks and dry and breakable vines, but at last Bramble saw Moonflower's feet swing up over the lip and vanish, and a moment later her hands were under his arm, helping him up after her.

He flopped onto his back on the lip of the ravine, catching his breath. The wildebeests below still roared, and he could hear the thunder of their hooves.

"They're on the move," said Mud's voice, and Bramble looked up to see the elderly baboon squinting down into the ravine. "Let's get out of here before they find a way to us."

"Grandmother must want us dead," said Bug.

"Or maybe she just wants to prevent us from getting back to Prance," said Moonflower darkly. "Either way, we must hurry. The smoke from the mountain was right: I fear Prance is in terrible danger. . . ."

CHAPTER FIFTEEN

Prance could barely make herself look at the carnage of the vulture pool, but she felt that it was her duty to bear witness, so that someone apart from Stormrider—and the shadow-flock—would remember.

The corpses all looked so small, in the flood of orange light from the dawn. They were nothing like the intimidating birds she remembered from her travels across the plains with Runningherd. It was as if they had shrunk to nothing more than sad piles of feathers when they'd been killed.

She stood among them, her shadow-form wavering with emotion, for as long as she could bear, and then she left. There was nothing she could do for them, not now, except find Grandmother and make her pay before she did something even worse.

She wandered over the mountainside, leaping lightly from

boulder to boulder at the speed of shadow, searching for any sign of the snake and the leopard who'd been with her.

She found the trail on a long, gravelly slope, close enough to the route she had taken to the elephant graveyard that Prance felt a shiver pass through her shadow-self. From high above, perched on a tall rock, she looked down at the slope and saw a pattern in the scree. A sinuous pattern of stones piling up, first on one side, then the other. The pattern of a huge snake's body slithering down the mountain.

Prance leaped from the mountain, following the trail, flashing from one side of it to the other. Even once the scree had ended, she could follow the path that they must have taken, trusting her instincts and her bird's-eye view as she hopped from the high branches of a baobab down to slipping through disturbed, head-high grasses. There was a small forest up ahead. Would they have circled around, not wanting to be slowed by the obstacle, or would they have gone through, welcoming the shelter from the open plain around it?

She stepped inside. The early morning light among the trees cast shadows almost as sharp and black as her own. She slipped between them, her hooves not quite disturbing the leaves underfoot, her shadow-ears twitching as she listened for hissing or growling. There was almost no sound, except for a very faint snoring coming from a clearing just up ahead. . . .

She stepped into the clearing and gasped. The whole floor of the clearing was covered with a huge, freshly shed snakeskin. She'd seen the one Bramble had found in the tunnel, but it was a different thing altogether to come upon this one lying where it'd been shed. Was it noticeably larger than the one Bramble had found, or was that Prance's imagination?

The source of the snoring was almost as frightening as the skin itself: a whole troop of vervet monkeys were lounging around the clearing, some up in the trees, but many of them snoozing in nests made from the coils of the skin. Prance *knew* they were cursed, even before she saw the first snakebite oozing on one of their shoulders. Only creatures who were under Grandmother's thrall would be so comfortable sleeping surrounded by her discarded skin.

She fled, slipping through the forest, before the encounter could turn into a repeat of her visit to the infected lions. She didn't want Grandmother to know she'd been there.

She went back to searching, but beyond the forest, the trail went frustratingly dead. The grass here was too short to betray Grandmother's movements, and there was no trace of the leopard either.

She woke up back in the Great Parent clearing with the early morning light streaming down on her, Gallant pacing from one side of the clearing to the other, and Stormrider and Moth all sitting within sight of her. All three of them were doing a good job of trying to look like they weren't watching her anxiously, but not so good that she didn't see them relax when she woke up.

Prance licked her lips and nibbled at the grass at her hooves. It wasn't the freshest, after days of being trampled by anxious animals coming to pay their respects to Thorn, but it helped.

Gallant started to hurry over to her and then froze, his ears twitching, and stared into the trees. Moth looked up too, following his gaze.

"Great Mother," Gallant said, slowly approaching Prance. "My pride has reported a strange scent. I can smell it now too—a creature I don't recognize. I've sent lions and baboons to search the forest, but so far we haven't found it."

"Sandtongue?" Prance asked, getting up and stretching her back.

"No, grasstongue—we think. It's strange." He looked up sharply once again, vigilance shining in his eyes, but a moment later a flock of small red birds took off from one of the trees, and he harrumphed and relaxed a little.

"I'm terribly thirsty," Prance said. "I was going to suggest going to the watering hole."

Gallant growled very softly, deep in his chest, and clawed at the ground at his paws. "I don't recommend it," he said. "We already know the watering hole's compromised, and now this. . . . I know we can't stay away from the water forever, but can it wait?"

Prance sighed. "I can't hide here," she said. "I need to show Bravelands I'm not afraid. Almost as much as I need to drink something."

"We'll go with you," said Moth. "Whatever it is, I'm sure Gallant and I can handle it."

Prance smiled at the young baboon as she sat up as tall as she could, bringing the top of her head up almost to the bottom of Gallant's chin.

Gallant growled again.

"I would prefer to wait until the rest of the pride returns," he said. "But we can go."

They moved slowly through the forest, Gallant stalking back and forth across the path ahead of Prance as they walked, Moth bringing up the rear with her eyes on the trees. Prance couldn't see, hear, or scent anything strange, so she tried to walk confidently, her head up, as if nothing was wrong—but it was hard to ignore the way Gallant's tail was swishing in front of her. However cautious the lion was by nature, he didn't worry like this without a good reason.

And since she no longer had the protection of a herd, she was grateful for all the eyes and ears on her side, whomever they belonged to.

But as the three of them emerged from the trees and set off across the open space toward the watering hole, suddenly she felt something. It wasn't the Us, but something gripped her heart, raising her pulse, and without even knowing what she was looking for, she turned her head.

One moment, she saw nothing but dappled shadows among long grass under a lone tree. The next, a big cat with a spotted pelt was flying across the plain toward her.

Prance turned and ran. She heard Gallant roar behind her and the thump of paws across the earth, but then there was nothing else in her mind but the running. Eyes fixed on the horizon, hooves throwing up hunks of grass, she leaped and swerved across the plain. Over a fallen branch and toward a muddy stream, panic and determination driving her into a pounding gallop—

Then pain flared in her rump. She felt skin tear, tried to get her hooves underneath her and just keep running, but the movement was agony, and she tripped and tumbled to the ground, the side of her face skidding in the mud.

It's not over.

The not-Us—the Great Spirit?—was clear and insistent in her head. *Get up!*

Prance rolled over as the leopard jumped for her, claws out. She managed to struggle to her hooves, leaving the big cat splashing in the shallow water. Prance tried to run, but she slipped, her right front hoof sinking deep into the mud. Blood was oozing over her flank, hot and terrifying, and her back legs were starting to wobble.

The leopard picked herself up and shook herself, scattering water into Prance's eyes.

"Wait!" Prance gasped, desperately.

There was a rumble like thunder, though the morning sky was clear and blue, and Prance was thrown to her knees in the mud as the ground underneath her quivered. The water around the leopard's paws churned and splashed, and the leopard's eyes suddenly turned fearful and uncertain. She backed out of the shallow river, walking unsteadily as the ground kept on shaking.

"What's happening?" the leopard cried. "What is this?"

The earth shivered, and then the quaking died away. Prance's legs were still trembling, pain and fear almost keep-ing her down—but she couldn't let them. With a heave and a grunt of effort, she dragged her hoof from the mud and managed to stand. She couldn't run, but while there was breath in her lungs, she wouldn't go quietly.

"Please," she said. "You don't have to do this."

The leopard's ears were flattened to her skull and she was looking around, confused and doubtful.

"I have no choice," Chase said. "I'm sorry. You're the one. The gazelle with no shadow. I have to hunt you, or my cub will die!"

Pounding pawsteps made Prance turn her head—but instead of a golden-maned lion, the creature that stomped into view like an unstoppable boulder rolling down a hill and knocked the leopard over on her back was large and black.

"Bramble!" Prance gasped.

Bramble hunkered down in front of her, planted both fists into the mud with a great *splosh*, and his shoulders heaved as he prepared to roar at the leopard. The leopard rolled back to her paws and into a crouch, hissing. . . .

"Chase?" Bramble said. "What are you doing here?"

"*Me?*" the leopard, Chase, yowled. "What are *you* doing here? You have to step aside, Bramble. I know you don't like violence, but I have to do this! I have to kill this grass-eater!"

"This grass-eater is Great Mother Prance," Bramble roared. "Great Parent of all of Bravelands, and I'll protect her with my life."

The lashing tail of the leopard went still and stiff, and Prance heard a sharp intake of breath. ". . . What?"

Prance was working on unsticking herself from the mud and limping painfully to drier land, keeping an eye on this strange reunion. Now Chase leaned to stare at her around Bramble's shoulder, and Prance tried to straighten up and look Great Motherly, even though her haunches were aching and her vision was swimming. Chase's eyes went wide and dark, and she backed away a couple of paces, shaking her head.

"Great Mother? But I . . . my cub . . . I have to . . ."

"Bramble, take her down!" came a roar, and at last Gallant thundered into view. There were claw marks across his nose. Prance flinched as she saw him, every bit the pride leader, flying across the grass with fury in his eyes. Chase flinched too—and then with a last yowl, she turned tail and fled.

Prance sat down heavily, her head spinning.

Gallant pursued Chase across the plain, neither of them slowing until they had both vanished behind the trees by the watering hole.

"Prance!"

Prance looked up to see the rest of Bramble's troop approaching. Moonflower was with her in a moment, and her strong hands were underneath Prance's ribs, helping her sit more comfortably. Mud wasn't far behind, despite his hobbling run, and soon he was sitting beside her, inspecting the torn skin where Chase's claws had caught her.

"You'll be all right," he said. "As long as you have time to heal. Bug, go and fetch the Goodleaf, right away."

One of the other baboons gave a nod and scampered off.

"You came back just in time," Prance said faintly.

Bramble and Moonflower exchanged a look.

"What?" Prance asked.

"Moonflower had a vision, in the smoke from the mountain," Bramble said. Pride and concern seemed to be fighting for control of his expression. "She knew you were in trouble. And we nearly didn't make it. Grandmother tried to stop us."

Prance took a deep, pained breath. "Tell me what happened," she said.

CHAPTER SIXTEEN

I think I've lost him. . . .

Chase stumbled to a halt and turned round and round on the spot a few times, scanning the horizon for any sign of the lion who'd chased her away from the gazelle.

No, not any gazelle. The Great Mother . . . I almost killed the Great Mother. . . .

But there was no lion. He must have finally tired out and given up, content that he'd driven her far from the gazelle with no shadow. And he had—she'd been running for what felt like half a day, and she wasn't sure where she was now, except that she was a little closer to the mountain again.

Chase took a few deep, panting breaths, and then flopped down on her side in the grass, staring at nothing, her chest heaving.

She lay there for a long time, her thoughts racing around her head as if the lion was still chasing them.

I should have realized there was nobody else Grandmother would want dead so much as the new Great Parent.

But who could have guessed that she would have been a gazelle?

This must be why Grandmother had made her kill that vulture—to find out if she would kill something defenseless and linked to the Great Spirit in order to save her own skin.

Chase licked at her sore paws and shuddered as she tasted the dusty remnants of the Great Mother's blood on her claws.

If the voice of the mountain hadn't stopped me, I would have killed her. What if she dies anyway? She looked so fragile!

How long until Grandmother knows what I've done—or haven't done? How long until her spies tell her I've failed her, and she kills Seek and Shadow?

Chase covered her eyes with her paw.

She had to save them. She had no idea how she could— lying here wouldn't help, but she was so tired.

Her stomach rumbled, and she realized she wasn't sure when she last ate. Everything since leaving the mountain was a blur of anxiety and sore paws.

Chase rolled over, staggered up onto all fours, and cast around. She was standing in thick grass, taller than she was in places, but when she climbed up onto a rock she could see in all directions, pale yellow and green plains stretching away. It wasn't *actually* endlessly flat—there were small hills, clumps of trees, rock formations, and trickling riverbeds—but Chase still felt lost among all this *distance*.

At least she could still rely on the sunset. She had run so long that the great fire in the sky was already tipping toward the horizon. She could follow it.

Her paws ached and her stomach squeezed as she prowled through the grass, alert for the sounds or scents of prey.

There must be a grass-eater on these plains that isn't the protector of all Bravelands, she thought, with a grim smile. Even exhausted and starving, she was still a leopard, still her mother's daughter. She would manage.

At last, she came to a rocky ridge and she smelled prey—not living creatures, but fresh blood and flesh. Drool filled her jaws as she crept closer and found that between the rocks there was a dark opening.

She hesitated, feeling as if she was being pulled in two directions at once—part of her never ever wanted to go back into any kind of underground cave again, not to mention that *something* had killed the prey in there, and it could be back at any minute. But her stomach was pulling her in, drawing her along the trail, and she couldn't deny it.

She stepped inside. The smell grew stronger as she ducked into the darkness between the rocks, and she struggled to control her drooling jaws. She would grab the prey, whatever it was, and drag it out and into a tree to eat. . . .

Her eyes adjusted to the dim light, and the prey in front of her . . . twitched.

She recoiled, and it was only then that she realized she'd been blinded by her hunger. The predators weren't on their way back.

They were already here.

A lion cub, half-grown, with a scruffy mane just starting to come through, was sitting in the darkness beside an elderly lioness with scars marring her face and her paws. Her tail was the thing that was twitching. The prey carcass was next to them, still unbelievably tempting, and for a moment Chase wondered if she could grab it and run. The scent made her throat tighten, every instinct telling her to go for it. But then the lioness's paw came down on the rib cage, and the cave was filled with a rattling chuckle.

"Well," said the lioness. "I think you've come into the wrong cave, young leopard."

"Sorry," said Chase.

"Yeah, get out," snarled the cub.

Chase was about to back out, when something stopped her. The old lioness wasn't just scarred and mangy—she was thin too, and there were fresh bite marks on her leg. Not like the snakebites she'd seen on the monkeys—this was the bite of a large predator.

What happened to these two?

She thought about leaving, about heading out to try to find her own prey, alone on the plains with no shelter.

The idea was not appealing.

"Please," she said. "I just need somewhere to rest. I don't want your prey."

The old lioness scoffed. The cub frowned.

"What happened to the rest of your pride?" Chase asked.

It was a guess, but she knew she'd gotten her claws into something when the lioness's chuckle turned into a growl.

"Do you think you're clever?" she snarled. "An old pile of bones like me and a half-grown cub, injured and alone? What could possibly have *happened*?" But after a moment, her mocking anger seemed to subside, and she gave an exhausted sigh. "My pride betrayed me. Useless bunch of rocks-for-brains. They all let themselves get bitten. The snakebites drove them mad. When we wouldn't let the snakes bite us too, they drove us out."

Chase glanced at the cub. His eyes were dark as he looked away.

"The sandtongue curse," Chase said. "Grandmother's influence is spreading. First monkeys, now lions . . ."

"Grandmother?" asked the cub.

"And what's your name, who knows so much about it?" grumbled the lioness.

"I'm Chase Born of Prowl," said Chase.

"My name is Menace, daughter of Titan," said the lioness. "This is Terror. We're all that's left of Menacepride."

Interesting names, Chase thought, but she kept that thought to herself.

"Well, Chase Born of Prowl, you might as well sit down, I can't be bothered to run you out of here now," said Menace. She started to clean her whiskers. "Tell us about this curse."

Chase took a deep breath, hardly sure where to start, but she told the two lions about the great snake who called herself

Grandmother, about the curse in the venom and what it felt like to be bitten, and about the remedy of consuming rot-meat.

"She wants to conquer *all* of Bravelands?" Terror asked, wide-eyed. He glanced up at Menace, who scoffed again.

"I wouldn't be too worried. If my father couldn't do it, I don't see why I should be afraid of some big worm."

"You haven't met her," said Chase darkly. "We must put our faith in the Great Spirit now."

"Huh! I don't put my faith anywhere but my own claws," Menace snarled. "Especially not in that wretched baboon who claims to be some sort of Great Father."

"The Great Father is dead," Chase said. "There's a new Great Mother now. A gazelle."

"A gazelle!" Menace rolled over, resting her head on the ground as she chuckled. For a moment she looked more like a gleeful cub than an elderly, injured old lioness. "Pathetic creatures, however tasty they are. What good is a gazelle going to be against cursed snakes? Maybe you *are* right to be worried."

"This one's different," Chase said. "Believe me, I know. She's protected by lions and gorillas—and she has no shadow."

"Oh, *that* gazelle," said Menace, to Chase's surprise. Her tail swished. "We've met it. It got *very* lucky. More than once. Maybe its luck will hold." She yawned hugely and laid her head down on her paws. "You can sleep here, if you want. Find your own prey in the morning."

"Thank you," said Chase. It wasn't what she was hoping for, but it would do. She relaxed into a sprawl, trying to ignore the delicious scent of the prey and just get some rest.

It was hard to forget about the meat, or about her hunger. Chase's stomach rumbled more than once, and she wondered if the two lions heard, or cared. After a little while, she heard the young lion begin to snore, and she sighed. She ought to try to get some sleep too; it wouldn't help her to be starving and exhausted. . . .

But before Chase could drop off, the old lioness spoke.

"Chase," she said. "I lied. You can have some of our food. Under one condition."

Chase almost leaped to her feet, completely awake and already salivating. But she forced herself to stay careful. She wasn't keen to make any more bargains, no matter how hungry she was.

Menace's tone was different. She wasn't laughing now. The haughty anger was gone. She sounded . . . mostly just very tired.

"What is it?" Chase asked warily.

"Take the cub with you. Take him back to his father."

"Your mate?" Chase asked, and Menace laughed again, a choked, rattling laugh that she suppressed quickly as Terror twitched in his sleep.

"Not on your life," she said. "No, he's not mine. I stole him from a lion called Gallant. Now it's time for him to go back."

"You *stole* him?" Chase whispered.

Menace gave her a long look. "I'm not a good lion," she said. "I never wanted to be, so I wasn't. But despite that . . . I have come to care for the cub. Very much. He won't get far without someone to look out for him, even though he's almost grown. Not in these dangerous times, without a mother or a father. He's not like me," she added with a rueful blink.

"And what about you?" Chase asked, although she could guess what the answer would be.

"My end is near," said Menace. "I've had a good life being a bad lion, but my leg's no use now. I don't think I'll leave this cave again."

Chase took a deep breath. She hated to refuse a last request, but . . .

"I don't think I can," she said. "There's something I have to do—I don't even know how to find where I'm going. He won't be safe with me."

"Safer than if he was all alone," Menace insisted.

Chase looked over at the half-grown lion, with his dark, scruffy mane and his gently twitching paws.

Don't give me another cub to care for, she thought. *I haven't exactly done a great job taking care of Seek. . . .*

But even as she thought of Seek, she knew she couldn't abandon Terror. Not if Menace was certain he wouldn't survive alone.

"All right," Chase said. "But you're going to have to explain it to him."

"Good," said Menace with satisfaction, and shoved the prey carcass across the stone toward Chase.

Chase dived in, unable to hold herself back. It was fresh

and delicious, and there wasn't a trace of rot on it anywhere.

But she'd taken only a few mouthfuls when she heard movement outside the cave. She looked up and saw that Menace was already dozing. Her heart sinking, she got up and slunk to the entrance.

Only a few steps from the outside world, she smelled reptilian blood and sour algae. She stopped, peering out into the darkness. She could hear the shuffling of their feet, their scaly claws and tails dragging across the rocks.

The shapes of their long muzzles began to appear through the gloom: four crocodiles, climbing up over the rocks and pressing into the entrance. Too late to run past them. The three big cats were trapped.

Chase backed away, pressing herself back into the cave.

"Crocodiles!" she yowled. "Wake up! Crocodiles!"

Terror was up and on his paws in a moment, his eyes wide, a growl building in his chest as the first of the snapping jaws poked through into their cave. Menace jolted awake too.

"Oh—oh, *good*," she growled. Chase looked around, uncertain if she was being sarcastic, but there was genuine, intense satisfaction in the old lion's black eyes. "Chase—get Terror out of here. I'll buy you some time."

"*How?*" Chase said, backing up against the rock wall of the cave as the crocodiles pressed in, one walking over the top of the other, snapping at Terror's paws.

"I won't leave you," Terror yelped, taking a wild swipe at the crocodile.

"You'll do as I say!" Menace roared, her voice filling the cave. Chase felt herself instinctively cower—even the crocodiles hesitated. And that was the pause that Menace needed. She bared her teeth, unsheathed her claws, and leaped on the crocodiles, clawing and biting. She sank a fang into the eye of one crocodile. Another snapped its jaws down on her back leg, and Terror let out a yelp of horror, but Menace barely winced— she kept fighting, dragging the crocodiles back into the cave with her, until the entrance was clear. Then she looked up and met Chase's gaze with a glare.

Chase nodded. It was now or never. She ran to Terror and headbutted him toward the cave entrance. He was too big for her to pick up and carry, but she could bodily push him over the tails of the crocodiles and out.

"No, Menace!" he cried as she shoved their way out into the cool nighttime air. "We have to go back for her!"

"We can't," Chase said, putting herself between him and the cave entrance. "She bought us time to get out, you have to respect that."

"But . . ." Terror's eyes were huge and full of sorrow as they stood outside the cave, panting and listening to the sounds of the fight. Yowls and hisses, thumps and scrapes, and above it all, the rattling sound of Menace's laughter. Chase could only imagine the violence that Menace was visiting on the crocodiles. They could hear her, defiant until the last moment, when the laughter died away, and there was only a shuffling and hissing from the cave mouth.

"Come on," Chase said, headbutting Terror once more.

"Menace *said* she wasn't a good lion, but she told me to keep you safe, and I'm going to. Follow me."

Terror stood frozen for a moment longer. Then he stumbled away, sticking close to Chase as she led him up and over the rocks and into the starlit plains.

CHAPTER SEVENTEEN

Bramble sat beside Prance, not wanting to go too far from her even though she was safely dozing in the Great Parent's clearing, her flank covered with a mixture of herbs that the baboon Goodleaf had brought to make sure her wounds would heal. She needed time to get better, and Bramble needed time to rest too—he just wasn't sure if any of them were going to get the time they needed.

"Hey, Bramble," said a voice. He turned to see some of the baboons, including Egg and Cricket Highleaf, standing nearby with distrustful looks on their faces. "I heard you let the leopard get away," said Egg. He squared up to Bramble, while Cricket hung back. "I would have thought you couldn't fail to catch her, with those huge fingers."

"Hey," said Moth in an angry whisper, hurrying up to them. "Not so loud! Great Mother's sleeping! Let's take this over there." She pointed to one of the tree stumps, where Moonflower was sitting with Bug and some of the other baboons, looking up at the stars.

Bramble glared at Egg but followed Moth over to the stump.

"So? What happened?" asked Cricket. "I heard you knew her name!"

"That part's true," said Bramble.

"Wait, what?" said Bug.

"I thought she looked like the kind of leopard we get on the mountain," Moonflower put in. "But by then she was being chased off by Gallant. . . ."

"It was Chase," Bramble said. "She lived on the mountain; her territory was near our troop. I don't know what she was doing down here."

"Just another creature under Grandmother's thrall, doing her dirty work," grumbled Gallant, loping up to the group and flopping down beside Moth. "I chased her a long way—she just kept running, no sign that she even knew where she was running to."

Bramble frowned down at his hands. He knew how it would sound to defend Chase when she'd almost killed the Great Mother . . . but none of the others had met her before, or seen the look in her eyes when he'd told her who Prance was.

"I don't know," he said. "I don't know why she thought she had to kill Prance, but I don't think she was infected. When I met her on the mountain, I thought all leopards were bad—I thought they'd killed my brother. But she saved me from a pack of hyenas. She had a strong spirit."

"Then why did she try to kill Prance?" Moonflower said.

Bramble just shook his head. He didn't know.

"The golden river," muttered a voice, and the gathered group turned to see Prance sitting up, her horns tipped back. A small bird was perched right on the tip of one of them, tweeting and bobbing its head. Prance's eyes were still closed, but she was muttering along with the bird. "The deep ravine, at the end of the golden river. Thank you, Pip."

The little bird bobbed its head again and then flew away. Prance opened her eyes and got up on all four hooves. She was a little wobbly, but Gallant rushed to her and let her lean against his flank.

"What's at the end of the golden river?" Bramble asked.

Prance blinked at him. "Grandmother," she said. "The birds have found her in the ravine. We can find it by following the river that catches the rising sun—that's what they mean by the golden river."

Bramble's hair stood on end, and he took a deep breath, trying to steady himself.

"What do we do?" he asked.

"We need to talk," said Prance. Her gentle face was drawn down into the most careworn expression Bramble had ever seen on her. "Let's go to Thorn's den."

Gallant began to help her along, and Mud and Moth both immediately followed, all four of them slipping through the branches to the sheltered spot where Thorn had always slept.

Bramble looked over at Moonflower, and at a nod from her,

they both started to make their way toward the hollow too. But Moonflower walked a little ahead, and when Bramble tried to follow her, a crowd of smaller shapes swung out of the trees or scampered in front of them, and Bramble jolted to a halt.

"Great Mother's advisers only," said Egg. "You're not one of them."

"But—" Bramble began.

"Don't you think you've done enough damage?" asked Cricket, glaring up at him.

Bramble felt cold and hot all at once. "I didn't—I was just trying to help," he said.

"You led Bug and Mango and the others off on a useless chase across the plains," said one of the other baboons, "and Mango didn't come back!"

"I . . ." Bramble opened his mouth and closed it again.

They were right. The whole thing had been pointless, and he'd gotten one of them killed. He was about to apologize, but the baboons didn't let him get a word in.

"And *then* you let the leopard go," said Egg, squinting suspiciously at Bramble. "After you tried to pretend to be the Great Parent! Maybe you secretly wanted her to get to Prance? Maybe you thought if she was out of the way, you could take her place?"

"No!" Bramble protested. "Listen, I only agreed to step up because Mud was so sure I was the one. I never asked to be Great Father!"

"We baboons don't take kindly to false Great Parents," said

Cricket, poking him hard in the ribs with one bony finger. "We won't let that happen again."

"Did you want it for yourself," sneered another baboon, "or are you working for Grandmother too?"

"Don't be stupid," Bramble growled. He wondered for a moment if he could simply brush these baboons aside and storm past them into the hollow. He probably could. But how would it help? "My sister's in there right now, you know. She's an outsider just like me!"

"Oh, and we're going to keep a close eye on her," said Egg. "But she's not the one who convinced Mud to pick her as Great Parent, and she's not the one who thought they could talk your mad father down. Is she?"

Bramble didn't dignify that with an answer. Frustration was building in his heart, and worse, it was building on a shaky ground suffused with guilt and doubt, like he was trying to stack stones in the middle of a flooding river. "All I've tried to do is help!" He bared his teeth in annoyance. Several of the baboons took shocked steps backward, and Bramble winced, regretting the gesture immediately.

"I think you should go," said Egg. "Before you do any more damage."

Bramble swallowed, hesitated, trying to think of something to say. But after a moment, he realized there was nothing. Not a single thing he could say to explain or apologize would convince any of these angry creatures.

So he stepped away.

He walked into the forest, not wanting to loiter uselessly

in the clearing while his sister and the others were talking to Prance. He put his head down and just knuckled along, shouldering through bushes and past trees, until he stopped at a tangle of tree roots and sank down into a hunched crouch. He traced patterns in the earth with one finger and thought about trying to sleep, but his mind felt like it was full of angry bees.

Prance would be fine. She had Moonflower, Moth, and Mud to advise her, not to mention Gallant to protect her. Gallant was the one who'd driven Chase away. The baboons weren't wrong. Bramble hadn't wanted to hurt her. But he was sure, deep down in the base of his stomach, that Chase hadn't known who Prance was, that there was something else going on with her, and that if they'd just been able to *talk*...

But maybe that was foolish. He'd convinced himself that he could talk to Burbark, and look how that had ended up.

Maybe action was what was needed.

The ravine at the end of the golden river, he thought. *That's where Grandmother is right now.*

What if even the time Prance and Moonflower were spending on planning would mean Grandmother was gone by the time they got there? What if she was preparing something too?

Bramble slowly stood up, looking up at the sky. The dawn wasn't here yet, but it would be only a little while longer.

What if he could end all of this now, just by doing something nobody saw coming?

* * *

The golden river was black and silver under the night sky, reflecting the moon as a faint shiver of light on the water, as Bramble walked along its bank. It had to be the right river: he'd set out from the forest in the direction he knew the sun would rise, moving toward the spot where he and Moonflower had tried to cross on the back of a hippopotamus and met Spider instead. This river ran toward the place where the sun would come up—not too long from now, from the faint tinge of gray on the horizon.

He told himself as he walked that he was sure he'd picked the right river to follow, but it was still a relief when the sound of trickling and splashing water grew louder, and the ground started to become mossy and rocky. He climbed up over the rocks and into a dark space under the branches of trees, as the river cut down into the earth, narrowing and deepening. At last, Bramble paused and looked down over the edge to see that the river was falling away into darkness in a thin waterfall.

This wasn't like the ravine where they'd fought the wildebeests. That had had gnarled trees and brown vines growing up the sides, but the cliffs had been far apart, the earth at the bottom open to the sky, wide and dry and flat from many years of trampling by the herds as they passed through.

Here the valley was much narrower, and the bottom lost in darkness beyond a wild green forest that seemed to cascade down the cliff face just like the waterfall. Trees grew from both sides, their branches meeting and tangling in the middle, so that the whole ravine was thick with shadow.

Grandmother was down there somewhere.

Hiding, he thought. *Lurking and waiting to make her next move. But there will be no next move.*

He clambered along the top of the ravine, among the dripping trees, feeling his way through the roots until he found a place where he thought he could begin to climb down. Wherever he chose to descend, he knew it would be risky: the shadows were so thick in the ravine that despite the dawn creeping up on the on the horizon, he could barely see beyond the next branch.

Slowly, carefully, he swung his legs over the edge and began to let himself down. He swung and clambered from tree root to rock to vine, making sure with every movement that he had a good grip, tensing as he lowered himself to the next branch and gently leaned his weight on it, holding his breath to see if it would creak or snap beneath him.

His mighty arms were soon stiff and burning with the effort of keeping his movements as quiet as possible, and he paused on a thick branch to catch his breath, peering down into the darkness. The sky above, when he squinted up through the thick canopy, was turning to a pale gray-blue. But something was strange about it.

Suddenly, he realized what it was. He could hear very faint chattering from the birds of Bravelands—but it was coming from far off, beyond the ravine. In the trees around him, through the whole ravine, not a single bird was singing.

Perhaps it's just too dark, he told himself, but his heart was beginning to beat faster as the eerie silence began to sink in.

He looked down, trying to see how much farther he had to go, but the bottom of the ravine was lost in a forest of branches and ferns. There seemed to be no sound except for his own breathing.

He couldn't stop now, no matter how frightening the descent was becoming. He had to make it to the bottom; he had to stop Grandmother before she could do anything else to hurt Bravelands. He gave himself a single, soft thump on the chest, to remind himself that he was strong, that he could do this. He slipped from the branch and lowered himself down to the next, and then onto a jutting rock ledge, and then into the roots of the same tree he'd rested in.

But as he was clambering through the roots, something happened. The branches he'd just left shivered above him, as if they were caught in a strong wind—but no wind blew through the ravine. For a moment, he thought that the birds had come at last.

But it wasn't birds that crept along the branches, dangling and then dropping to land in the roots beside him. It was snakes. The tree, the roots, the cliff was *full* of snakes. Black, gray, green, large and small, ones that rattled, and ones that opened their mouths as long, dripping fangs folded out of their upper jaws.

Nowhere was safe. Shuddering and yelping, Bramble tried to climb out onto another branch, but his hand came down on what he thought was a stick and found it soft and yielding and scaly. He pulled it away, couldn't keep his balance, and he fell— but he didn't drop into empty air. Instead, a huge green snake curled tight around his ankle and caught him, dangling him upside down over the drop. He gasped in a terrified breath as the ferns swung underneath him, then tried to reach up and claw at it, but he couldn't bend himself up to get his fingers around the snake's body. He wriggled and tried to swing himself to another branch, and then the world tumbled over and over as he dropped, caught himself on a vine, which snapped. He landed with a thump and a groan, in the crook of a tree not far from the ground. Winded, panicked, and with snakes crawling up from below and dropping down on him from above, he tried to force himself to get up and run. He rolled rather than climbed out of the tree and down to the ground, landing in cold water—the stream, running down from the waterfall above. It wasn't deep, but he slipped and slid on the mossy rocks trying to clamber out, and then tripped and fell onto his knees as something heavy dropped down onto his neck and shoulders. The huge green snake again, but this time it was around his waist and around his neck, pinning his arms, choking him.

He clawed at the snake, but it tightened so fast that his vision swam and he couldn't get a grip on the smooth scales. He knelt in the cold water, his vision swimming, gasping for breath. His head throbbed along with the painful hitching of his chest. He wrenched at the snake with weakening fingers, lost his balance, and fell back into the shallow water. Black shadows flickered across his vision as the snake curled tighter and tighter.

One of the shadows was moving down the waterfall, leaping

and swinging and slipping down the rocks.

Moonflower.

She was almost at the bottom. She was sprinting down the stream toward him, reaching for him.

The snake gave one last twist, and Bramble's whole body convulsed as the breath was squeezed from him. The last thing he saw was his sister's outstretched hand, before everything went black.

CHAPTER EIGHTEEN

"Read them again," said Gallant.

"There's no point," muttered Moth. "I can see . . ."

"There has to be something else," Gallant protested.

"No, Moth's right," said Mud, leaning heavily on the ground. "We see the same thing, there's no doubt."

All three of them were sitting around the Starleaf's stones, staring at them as if maybe *this* time they would say something different—but Prance sat a little apart. Mud was right. For once, both baboons agreed completely on what they'd seen, and what it meant. There was no point questioning it. She didn't have time. She had to decide what to do about it.

A sudden nightfall, blocking out the sun. Birds falling from the sky, earth swallowing the trees. The watering hole turned to a lake of fire.

"If that's all really coming, we should get Great Mother away from here," said Gallant. "We should *all* get away. Round up every animal we can find and leave."

"And go where?" Prance said, her heart heavy. "Out of Bravelands? How far should we go? In what direction? Is anywhere safe if Grandmother can block out the sun?" She shook her head. The Great Spirit was quiet within her; the spot where Thorn had touched her heart felt tingly and cold. "Anyway, we couldn't possibly bring every animal in Bravelands with us. We couldn't find them, and half of them wouldn't come. What kind of Great Mother would I be, if I didn't fight for *all* the creatures of this place?"

"Yeah!" Moth said. The others looked at her sternly, and she shrank a little. "Well, she's right. Great Father Thorn didn't flee from Titan, did he? There must be a way to save Bravelands from all of this."

Prance wished that Bramble and Moonflower were here to help her think. They knew the gorillas, they knew where this had all started—she was sure they had a role to play, if only she could think what it was. But Bramble hadn't come in to talk, so Moonflower had gone to find him. She hoped they'd be back soon. . . .

"Perhaps we simply kill the snake," said Gallant darkly. "She is large and fierce, but she must be mortal."

Prance closed her eyes.

Great Spirit, can you help me? Spirits of my ancestors, of the Great Parents of the past, is Gallant right? Is there no other way?

The Great Spirit stayed silent within her, but something was holding her back.

Perhaps it was just her own heart.

"It would be within the Code," she admitted, opening her eyes slowly. "She threatens the survival of us all. I'm not saying that it would be *wrong*... but I don't think I can do it. Not yet."

"Then when?" said Gallant. Prance looked up at him, and he looked away quickly.

"When I know there's no other choice," she said. "I will try to speak with Grandmother directly. I know there's not much hope, but the point of a Great Parent is to have someone to listen, to deliberate, to *compromise*. Perhaps there's something neither Grandmother nor I have thought of that will save us all. The only way I can find out is to ask."

"But you can't go to her," Moth said, shuddering. "She's *huge*. She'll roll over you and crush you like an ant without even thinking, and that's if she doesn't bite your head off before you can even see her."

"You're not wrong," Prance admitted. "But I won't be going in my physical form. Grandmother can see me. Just like you can, when I'm in my shadow-form. If I visit her that way, she shouldn't be able to hurt me."

"We won't be able to go with you," Mud pointed out. "You'll have to face the snake all alone."

"I understand that," said Prance. "But I'm willing to risk it. I must try."

Moth, Mud, and Gallant looked at one another, and Moth rushed up to Prance and threw her arms around her neck.

"We'll be right here," she said.

Prance nodded, touching her nose to the side of Moth's head. Then she stepped out of her body, leaving it to sink to a sitting position in Thorn's hollow.

There was no time to waste. She flickered through the forest, flowing through the shadows. The river was starting to turn gold as the sun rose, and she cantered along beside it until she saw the steam rising from the rock walls where the waterfall cascaded into the ravine. She rose into the sky to look at the ravine from above. The green canopy obscured any sight of the bottom, and the ravine went a long way. From here, Prance's breath caught as she realized she could see patterns in the land that she would never have noticed from the ground —she could trace the line of the ravine and the river through cliffs, rock formations, and streams, all the way back to the foothills of the mountain.

She knew of the ravine from her travels with the herd—they had seen it from afar and avoided it carefully. It was no place for gazelles, with their delicate legs. They preferred the open plains, where the Us could take them far from danger.

The Us would be screaming at me not to go in there, she thought. *But the Great Spirit knows I must.*

She made her way down, slipping between the branches of the trees, feeling reassured to be just one shadow among so many. She was about halfway down when she started to notice the snakes. They didn't seem to see her—they just hung listlessly over every branch, curled up in the cracks between the rocks. Lizards with glassy-eyed stares flicked their tongues at her as she descended.

At last, she began to hear noises—like the snuffling of the vervet monkeys, but much louder and deeper. Soon, she came upon the source of the sound: gorillas, dozens of them, sleeping in heaps among the ferns or in the trees. She walked between them, her heart racing, trying to keep her head high.

In the center of the sleeping gorillas, she found a shaft of dim light filtering through the trees and gleaming on dark black and red scales.

Grandmother stirred. She raised her head, towering over Prance just as she'd towered over Thorn when they'd visited her before he died. Her head was turned a little to one side, and Prance realized that there was something wrong with her left eye. It was half-closed and looked as if it was filmed over with some milky substance.

Good morning and welcome, she said, her tongue flicking out to taste the air, uncomfortably close to Prance's shadow-horns. *So the Great Parent lives. We have that in common, you and I. Other creatures may assume that we are weak, but we can show our strength when needed, can't we?*

"We can," Prance said. She took a deep breath and looked into the great snake's gleaming black eye. "I don't know why you feel you need to do this, Grandmother," she said. "To take over other creatures and control their minds. Perhaps the sandtongues haven't been treated as they should by the other creatures, but this—this can't be the answer. If you tell me your complaints, and you let these gorillas and all the other creatures go, I will help you with whatever it is you need. The Great Spirit will welcome you, all your kind, if you can keep to the Code—only kill to survive."

Only kill to survive, Grandmother repeated. For a moment,

Prance thought she was actually considering it, but then the snake shook her head, a strange echoing laughter sounding in Prance's mind. *What pathetic creatures you are. To fetter yourselves to this 'Great Spirit,' to let it dictate your every moment. I do not come here simply to right some wrong, and I am not interested in your help.*

She rose up even taller, her head swinging from side to side.

I will give you a chance to run, little shadow, she said. *But I do not offer mercy. Already the ground of Bravelands trembles in my presence. I come to bring a new era, where the Great Spirit will be dust under my scales.*

"The creatures of Bravelands will not go quietly into that future," said Prance. "The Code allows them to defend themselves. Even if you win in the end, you will lose many of your followers. . . ."

Grandmother scoffed. *The creatures who follow me are expendable, like one of my skins: I will shed them as easily if it means I bring destruction down on you and your pathetic grasstongue herds. The Code under my rule will be Kill, and You Shall Thrive!*

Prance concentrated on breathing calmly as she listened to this, keeping her eyes on Grandmother's face as the words washed over her. She found that yes, she was afraid; everything Grandmother said was frightening. But the Great Spirit seemed to stir within her, as if all the Great Parents she'd seen at the watering hole were with her now, waiting to see how she would respond.

She looked into Grandmother's face. "Is there anything at all I can say to make you relent?"

I told you, NO, Grandmother hissed.

"Because if not," Prance said, her voice steady, "then it will be war. I would take any other path before I led Bravelands into bloodshed, but if I have no choice then I will do it."

You have no choice, said Grandmother. *And there will be no war. If any stand in my way, it will be a massacre. And you will be responsible, Prance Herdless. You are marked to die. You know that, don't you? Your spirit fled your body on the day you found yourself without a shadow. Now it lingers here, and while it does, it will be the work of a moment for my followers to sever it from your fragile body.*

Prance froze. She could feel the hair standing up all along her back, even though her body was a long way away. She took a breath, looking up at the bloodthirsty expression of triumph in Grandmother's glistening eye.

Then she blinked herself back into her body, and she heard growling. When she opened her eyes, Gallant's tail was swishing in front of her face as he stood over her, Moth and Mud beside her holding rocks and sticks, while all around the hollow there paced a pride of gaunt, scarred, mean-looking lions.

"Menacepride," growled Gallant.

"We come from Grandmother," slurred one of the lions. "We bring you the gift of death."

CHAPTER NINETEEN

"Where are we going?" Terror asked, and not for the first time.

They were climbing the side of a kopje, one of the small densely green hills that rose sharply out of the plains.

"We're going to find my cub," Chase said again. "And my friend Shadow."

"You said that before," Terror grumbled. "But you won't tell me where they are. . . ."

Chase rounded on him. The roar died in her throat as she saw his worried, uncertain face. "That's because . . . I don't know," she said. "They were taken. I don't know where. I can't stop, or they'll be killed. They might be dead already. I don't know."

Terror's ears went back, and he hung his head.

"Oh. Sorry," he said.

Chase sighed.

"I should have told you. I just hoped . . . well, I'm going up this tree," she said. "If I can see out over the plains, I . . . I hope I'll see *something* that can help me find them."

"All right. I'll keep watch here," said Terror, and sat down in the roots of the tree. Chase felt a rush of gratitude. Terror could have chosen to run off on his own, no matter what Menace said.

You really weren't named very well, she thought. *What would be a good lion name? Something like . . . Fortitude? Or Loyal. Loyal would be a good name.*

"Thanks," she said.

She ran up the huge baobab tree in a few long bounds and walked out onto one of the thick, topmost branches. She scanned the plains, looking for Shadow's black form, or for a group of gorillas, or even Grandmother herself slithering through the grass. But apart from the smoke rising from the mountain, there was nothing out of the ordinary. . . .

Except then she looked down and saw with a jolt that there was a pack of hyenas making right for the kopje. Chase tensed. A whole pack, nine or ten of them—Terror would put up a good fight, but there was no doubt who would win. Even with Chase there, it didn't even the odds much.

She dropped down out of the tree beside Terror and nudged him with the top of her head.

"We have to go."

"I smell hyenas," Terror said nervously.

"That's right," Chase said. "They're coming up that way, come on, let's go back down—we can outrun them on flat ground." *Probably*, she added, to herself. *We can* probably *outrun them.* . . .

They snuck away, creeping around the huge baobab, through the ferns and between boulders, down to the base of the kopje, and then —

"Well, well," said a snarling voice.

Chase froze, her hackles raising. Two hyenas were standing right in front of her, black manes bristling down their backs, their doglike faces alight with amusement. They must have sprinted around the hill to get here ahead of them. Chase snarled at them, backing up close to Terror, as the bushes on either side of them started to rustle, and the yipping laughter and smell of hyena breath told her that they were surrounded.

"Don't come any closer," she said. "Or you'll regret it."

"He-heh," said a hyena, stepping out from behind a bush in front of Chase, "I think we've already had this conversation more than once, haven't we?"

Chase stared at the large female who stood before her, one torn ear twitching in amusement.

"*Ribsnapper?*"

Chase stepped forward, sniffing carefully. It *was* Ribsnapper, the hyena who'd helped her learn about the rot-meat cure for the sandtongue curse. Chase had saved her once, and she'd saved Chase in return. She'd even helped her rescue Seek from the gorillas.

But . . . what did that mean for them right now? Hyenas were ruthlessly, *notoriously* likely to forget about past friendships if they were desperate enough for a meal. . . .

"You're a long way from the mountain," Ribsnapper said. She seemed friendly enough, though Chase couldn't help looking over her shoulder to the faces of her pack, and she didn't like the way they were looking at her and Terror.

"I could say the same for you," Chase said.

Terror's hackles were rising, his paws treading the ground as if he wasn't sure whether to run or attack.

"Well, you must have left before the tremors began," Ribsnapper said. She sat down and scratched behind her ear with one back paw. "They got so bad, I decided to leave. You couldn't keep your footing, or hardly breathe for the smoke from the vents up there now. Bad smells. Bad omens. So I left. Found a new pack down here on the plains." Ribsnapper looked over her own shoulder, saw the hyenas there drooling, and let out a snappy bark. "Hey! Don't look at them like that. They're not for eating." She lashed out, catching the closest hyena a stinging blow across the muzzle. The hyena yelped and dropped his head in supplication, and Chase relaxed a little at last.

"Chase," said Ribsnapper, turning back to her with a solemn look on her face, "I'm sorry about Shadow and Seek."

Chase blinked. "What do you mean? Did you see them get taken?" Her heart began to beat faster. If the hyenas knew where they'd been taken to, then—

"No," said Ribsnapper solemnly. "I only saw the bodies."

Chase's heart stopped. Her paws almost slipped out from underneath her.

"What?" she whispered.

"Oh, Chase . . . did you not know?" Ribsnapper scratched at the ground sadly. "We saw them not far from here."

"Where?" Chase snapped. "Show me."

Perhaps there'd been some mistake. Perhaps Ribsnapper had only seen them sleeping, or . . .

Hyenas know when something's dead, a voice in her head told her, but she shook it off. There was still a chance. There *had* to be a chance. It couldn't end like this.

And if it had . . . she could never rest unless she saw it for herself.

"I'll take you there," Ribsnapper said. "Come on."

Chase hated how gentle the hyena's voice had become. She hated the space that the other hyenas gave her as she followed Ribsnapper down the slope and onto the plains. She almost wished that she could go back to being afraid of them. She hated the blue sky above, and the fact that she couldn't quite feel her paws or stay in a straight line as she walked. She hated how *close* they were, and how if Ribsnapper hadn't come along she might never have found them, even though they were so close.

The sun had barely moved in the sky when they came across the small watering hole, crowded around with bushes and rocks, with the small, flat island in the center, and saw the two motionless shapes lying on the island.

There was no mistake. Shadow and Seek lay together, legs stiffly out beside them, unmoving.

Chase's legs gave out and she sank to the ground.

Ribsnapper was saying something, but Chase felt as if

the sight of the bodies was deafening her. She couldn't hear a thing apart from her breath stalling in her throat and her heart rattling in her ears, until Terror's voice broke through the fog:

"I think the cub's breathing!"

"What?" Chase looked up as the lion cub charged into the water. The splashes from his big paws flew all around, striking her in the face, and she felt as shocked and breathless as when she had plunged headfirst into the waterfall outside Range's cave. Terror reached the island, with Ribsnapper close on his heels, and started to paw at Seek's small body.

"Chase!" Ribsnapper called back. "Spinebreaker, Furripper, bring her, quick!"

Chase jolted back to her paws as two of the hyenas drove their muzzles under her sides and shoved her toward the island. She ran, splashing through the water, and clambered up onto the shallow bank beside Seek just in time to see Shadow's eyes flicker open.

"Chase . . . ," he said weakly, his chest hitching. "No . . ."

"What do you mean, *no*?" Chase said. She was so happy and confused to see him alive that she thought she might bite him. She turned to Seek and nudged him with her muzzle, and the cub let out a weak groan. It was the best sound she had heard in all her life.

"They said you'd come," Seek whispered.

"Who did?" said Ribsnapper. But Chase didn't need to ask. She stood over Seek protectively and raised her head.

"It's a trap," groaned Shadow.

And sure enough, black shapes were clambering slowly over the rocks, all around the watering hole. The pointy black heads and huge, muscular arms of gorillas, all of them staring right at Chase with the glassy gaze of the cursed.

They slipped into the water from the bank and from the rocks, wading toward the island in a slow march, like ants converging on their anthill.

Chase extended her claws and raked them through the earth.

"You should not have betrayed Grandmother," the gorillas said, speaking in near unison. "Now all three of you will die."

CHAPTER TWENTY

Prance backed up against the high rock of the Great Parent clearing, her heart racing. There was a moment of awful quiet, as the lions of Menacepride stared at her with hungry eyes. They weren't even looking at Gallant, who trod the ground in front of her, tense, waiting for one of them to move. At last, Moth let out a yell of frustrated rage and threw her stone at one of the lions. It struck true, right in the middle of its nose, but the lion barely flinched.

Then they all moved, as one. Gallant leaped at them, batting and snapping, knocking one lion to the ground and then another—but there were too many, and they were being driven by something straight toward Prance. They either ignored Gallant's attacks or walked right into them, and he couldn't stop them all.

Mud and Moth jumped onto the back of one of them and

clawed at his eyes, stopping him in his tracks.

Prance screamed and jutted her horns toward the first lioness who came within reach, tossing her head desperately through the air, feeling them catch on her fur. But the lioness was too big, and Prance was tripped and knocked to the ground on her back, kicking frantically with her hooves even as the lions stood on her neck and her rib cage, preparing to rip out her throat.

Then another furious roar rang out, and the lion standing on Prance's neck was thrown aside, its claws tearing her skin as it fell. Another lioness came into view, healthier fur and eyes blazing with fury. "Take them down!" she commanded, and Prance managed to clumsily push herself up and press herself against the rock again.

Gallantpride was bursting into the hollow, tearing through the sheltering bushes that hadn't already been broken by Bramble's fight with the lizard. Valor led them, her fur bristling with rage.

Even with more even numbers, the fight did not end quickly. Menacepride was swarming over Gallant, blood and fur flying, impossible to tell which lion they belonged to. Gallantpride rushed to back up their leader, throwing the infected lions off him, snapping and roaring—but Menacepride wouldn't retreat, not even when Valor and Gallant had killed one each and the tide of the battle was turning. They kept staring at Prance, even as the other lions were bearing them to the ground. Even as Valor's teeth closed in the neck of a mangy-looking lioness, her eyes were fixed on Prance, and the murderous hatred lingered in them until they rolled back in her head.

Prance slowly backed up, trying to get out of the way and give the warring lions space. But as she slipped out through a gap in the bushes, she almost tripped over the fallen, panting form of a Menacepride lion. He was wounded, blood pouring from a claw mark across his eye, but he looked up, and his one working eye fixed on Prance. He struggled to his paws and took a swipe at her, which she danced around with a bray of alarm.

"Prance, run!" cried Moth's voice, but Prance couldn't see her. She skittered away, giving the lion a wide berth, heading into the clearing. She could hear the lion behind her, grunting with pain, paws thudding unevenly but faster and faster. She burst out into the open space, sprang up and over the first of the tree stumps, and then heard a snap and a crunch. She skidded to a halt in the leaves and looked around.

Sky the elephant matriarch had been standing in the clearing, too still for Prance's panicking mind to even notice, but now there was a limp lion's body impaled on one of her tusks. With a disgusted grunt she tossed her head, dislodging the body and throwing it to the ground.

"Are you all right, Great Mother?" she asked.

Prance couldn't answer for a moment. Her knees turned wobbly, and she sank down in the grass.

"Gallant," she managed to say. "There were more of them. They're behind the rock. . . ."

Sky frowned and pressed her huge head in through the

trees, shouldering one aside so that it bent over, shedding leaves and fruits.

Prance heard her say something, though she wasn't sure what it was. Then Sky pulled out of the trees again and lumbered over to Prance.

"Gallant is all right," she said. "It's over now."

"I went to talk to her," Prance said. "I offered her help, reconciliation . . . anything to save Bravelands. But she wouldn't take it. She sent the lions. And now there's going to be blackness and fire, and . . . I don't know what to do, Sky. I can't fight a war."

"Not on your own," Sky said, laying her trunk gently over Prance's back. "But you're not alone."

From behind her, the lions of Gallantpride were emerging from the trees. Gallant himself looked distinctly shaken, walking with a limp, with more than one bleeding wound in his flank. Valor was only a little better off. Mud and Moth were both with them, Moth wearing a quickly swelling lump on her head and an expression of grim satisfaction.

"We won," she said. "But it seems like Grandmother was not very receptive to peace talks," said Moth.

"That was just the beginning," said Prance.

Gallantpride settled in the clearing all around Prance, licking their wounds. She tried to think of something to say to them. How could she tell them that war was on the horizon, and that she wasn't even sure it was a war they could win?

A gasping cry split the air, and Prance's head whipped around.

"Help!" came the voice. "Please, help me!"

Gallant leaped unsteadily to his paws, Valor beside him, as a lumpy black shape came through the trees and collapsed at the edge of the clearing.

"Moonflower!" Prance sprang to her hooves and was by the gorilla's side in a few strides, with Moth right behind her. Moonflower flopped to the ground, and Bramble rolled from her back and sprawled in the grass, unmoving.

"What happened? Moth touched her small hands to Bramble's face, prying open his eyes, pressing her ear to his chest.

"Snakes," Moonflower gasped. "He went . . . to the ravine . . . I was too late. . . . I carried him back. . . . Please . . ."

Moth looked up at Prance, and Prance's heart felt cold. There was grief welling in the baboon's eyes.

"He, h-he can't be dead," Moonflower wailed. "Please, I made it back, please, Bramble . . ."

She crumpled into a furry heap, sobbing, ripping up grass in great leathery handfuls.

"He's not breathing, Prance," Moth sniffled.

"*Prance . . . ,*" a voice echoed.

She twitched, turning to look back the way that Moonflower had come . . . and she saw a shadow there, among the trees, standing with his large arms hanging loose and his head tilted to one side. He was pure shadow, and she couldn't see his face, but she felt his confusion as he stared across the clearing at his own body lying motionless in the grass.

"Bramble," Prance said. The shadow-form—the spirit of Bramble—paused for a moment and then took a step backward, into the trees. Prance's heart skipped a beat. "No, don't go!" she cried. "Moth, it might not be too late. Is there anything you can do if a creature's not breathing? Anything at all?"

"I—I'm not a Goodleaf," Moth stammered.

"Stand aside! I know what to do!"

Spider was swinging through the trees toward them, with the desperate speed of a much younger baboon. He dropped to the ground beside Bramble's body with a groan, balled his hands into fists, and brought them down hard on Bramble's chest with a dull thud.

"What are you doing?" Moonflower gasped.

"Saw this," Spider said, and raised his fists again and brought them down hard. "With the chimpanzees. One fell in the water, couldn't breathe. This woke up its spirit! Trust me."

"It *is* working," Prance breathed. She kept her eyes on Bramble's spirit as Spider drove his fists into his chest—every time he did, the shadow took a hesitant step forward, toward Prance, back toward his own body. "Come on, Bramble, you can do it," she told him. There was a tense, worried silence as Spider pressed down on Bramble's chest, as hard as he could, and when his arms started to shake, Moth took over, and all the while Bramble himself was knuckling closer.

"Prance—Prance, what are you looking at?" Moonflower asked suddenly.

"Come on," Prance whispered, not breaking her stare at Bramble. He was so close now. "Come on, you can do it."

Moth gave another great heave into Bramble's chest, and

the shadow shuddered and vanished. Prance startled, looking around. Had he gone, fallen at the final step? Had Bramble died?

Then, on the ground, Bramble's body convulsed, and he took in a long, terrible, rattling breath.

Moonflower gave a cry of joy and shock and reached for her brother, patting and holding his shoulders, helping him roll onto his side and then press up onto shaking arms.

Bramble sat there coughing and panting for some time, and then he looked up—first at Moonflower, who pressed her forehead to his so hard Prance could almost hear their heads knock together, and then at Prance.

She couldn't read his expression—his eyes were watery and unfocused. Did he remember being a spirit? Did he know that she'd been able to see him?

"Spider, you crazy old baboon, you did it," said Mud, coming over and slapping his old friend on the back.

"Spider knows things," said Spider, with a smugness that made Mud roll his eyes.

There was a rumble of thunder in the distance, and Prance looked up, expecting to see gray clouds gathering and sense rain in the air. But the sky was blue . . . except that above the treetops a huge plume of black cloud was rising. She stared.

No. Not now. It can't be happening already. . . .

Then there was another rumble, much louder, much less like thunder, and the ground underneath her hooves began to shake. Every creature in the clearing crouched and let out yelps of surprise and fear as the trembling grew and then subsided.

Mud stepped up to Prance and put his hand on her side, following her gaze to the black cloud as it spread farther and farther into the sky.

"It's happening," he said. "Just as the stones said."

"Then there's no time to lose," said Prance.

CHAPTER TWENTY-ONE

Chase prowled around the island, facing each approaching gorilla in turn, her tail swishing.

"You don't want to do this," she snarled. "I have Ribsnapper and Terror on my side."

"They will not save you," said the gorillas, in their eerie chorus. Chase shuddered.

"And what about my pack?" Ribsnapper yipped.

The gorillas' relentless approach paused. As one, they looked over their shoulders.

"Now!" Ribsnapper commanded, and from hiding places all around the watering hole the hyenas emerged, snarling and giggling. Chase's heart raced as they splashed into the water like excitable, ferocious pups.

Not sure how they feel about me, but it's clear how these hyenas feel about an opportunity for a fight! she thought.

Throwing back her head in a howl, Ribsnapper leaped into the water too, clamping her jaws down on the arm of the nearest gorilla. He reeled, grabbed the back of her neck, and tried to pull her off, but her teeth just dug deeper in.

There was a splash and a thump right behind Chase and she spun around and saw one gorilla had slipped between the hyenas and was stomping up onto the island, thick fingers reaching for Seek's neck. Chase roared and clawed at its face, sending it reeling back into the water. She snarled, snapped, and dodged the gorilla's swinging fist as it sailed over her head, but the other fist slammed into her shoulder and sent her rolling over into the water.

Chase heard Terror roaring and the hyenas yapping before her head was plunged under the surface, and for a moment there was just the sound of water in her ears and her own heart thumping. Then she scrambled around, burst from the water in a shower of droplets, and bit down on the gorilla's knee, trying to drag it back with her. It screamed and flailed, and its fingers found Chase's jaws—to her horror, it was so strong that it prized her jaws open. The muscles in her face twitched and ached, and she let go, afraid if she kept on trying to bite down the gorilla would rip her jaw from her face.

She raked her claws across its side, blood seeping into the water, and then there was a sound that rolled over the watering hole and made Chase's heart stutter. It sounded a bit like thunder, and a *lot* like the rumbling sound that had stopped her from hurting the Great Mother. Chase backed away from the gorilla up onto the island. Seek and Shadow were still safely there in the center, huddling close to each other, Shadow curled completely around Seek. Terror was standing over them, looking terrified and desperate, and all of them were staring up into the sky.

The gorillas and the hyenas looked up too, the gorillas in a slow and eerie unison, the hyenas with anxious and confused yaps. Chase's gaze was drawn toward the mountain, which loomed huge and dark beyond the foothills.

Then the ground shook, and the water shivered around the fighting animals. Chase caught her breath as she saw the gorillas turn and flee, stomping through the water, ignoring the hyenas who'd stopped their onslaught to steady themselves against the earthquake.

Then the mountain exploded. Black smoke belched into the sky, followed by great gouts of orange flame, or . . . *was* that flame? It was too far to make out any detail, but *something* was raining down over the forest at the top of the mountain, not the delicate flickering of a flame, but something heavy and bright. . . .

Like the leopards in the stories, Chase thought, although she didn't think that those were leopards being flung from the tip of the mountain into the sky.

"Cowards," Ribsnapper spat at the retreating gorillas, clambering out of the water to Chase's side. "Come on. We should get away from here. Can they walk?" She nudged Shadow with one paw.

"I'll take Seek," Chase said. Her cub was only just still small enough to be carried by the scruff, but it was better than asking him to walk. "Shadow, can you make it?"

"I think so," said Shadow. "I can't believe you did it . . . Chase . . ." He started trying to get up weakly, his legs shaking.

"It wasn't all me," Chase said, with a grateful look at Ribsnapper, and then a worried one up at the mountain, where the smoke was still flowing into the sky, expanding into a dark and heavy-looking cloud.

They managed to get Shadow off the island, Terror and Ribsnapper taking up positions on either side to catch him if he fell. But he made it to solid land, and they rested in a heap together, the hyenas panting and grumbling to one another as they stared at the spreading black cloud.

"What does it mean?" Ribsnapper said.

"It's going to cover the sun in a moment," Terror added in a frightened murmur.

Chase's fur shivered, starting behind her ears and running all the way down to her tail and back. She shook herself with a small yowl.

"This is bad," she muttered. "It's really bad. There's something she said. Was it . . . the fire snakes? No, it . . ."

"What's she on about?" one of the other hyenas muttered to Ribsnapper, and got a nip on the ear in reply.

"*When the sun no longer shines in the daytime*," Chase said. She looked up at the hyenas, then down at Shadow and Seek, her heart feeling like it was falling into a deep pit. "It's Grandmother. This, *this* is her plan!" She looked up at the cloud again. How far until it reached the sun? Not far enough. "I have to go," she said.

"*Go?*" Terror gasped. "What do you mean, go where?"

"Grandmother's shedding. She told me the sun would go dark in the middle of the day and that's when she'd lose her skin, one last time. If I don't stop her now, there'll be no stopping her ever again."

"You can't go alone," said Shadow. He stood up and leaned his head against her.

"Are you strong enough?" Chase asked.

"They starved us," said Shadow. "If I can eat something, I'll be fine. It was hard enough to be parted from you the last time," he added, his voice low. "I won't do it again now."

Chase took a deep breath, her heart beating even faster as Shadow's dark eyes looked into her own.

"We've stashed some prey in the trees just that way," Ribsnapper said. Several of the hyenas groaned, and Ribsnapper turned on them. "No arguments! You all just half drowned yourselves fighting gorillas to rescue this leopard—you want him to starve now?"

There were still a few grumbles from the hyena pack, but none of them spoke up.

"Thank you," Chase said. "Ribsnapper—you've already done so much for me, but will you and your pack take Seek and Terror to the Great Mother?"

"What?" said Terror. "You're going to leave us here with these . . ." He didn't finish the thought, but he looked around at the hyenas with wide eyes.

"I'm leaving you with the Great Mother," Chase said. "They're just going to get you there."

"It's okay," said Seek, in a small voice. "Ribsnapper looked after us before. I trust her."

Ribsnapper chuckled and lowered her face to sniff at Seek. "And usually that would be a terrible decision," she said. "But in this case, I give my word—on the Great Spirit, and on the Great Devourer itself. No harm will come to the cubs."

"Then we need to go," Chase said, casting another look into the sky at the huge, expanding cloud.

"Go," said Ribsnapper.

Chase gave Seek a last lick on the forehead. "I love you. Be good. Look after Terror for me."

Terror stared down at the much smaller leopard cub with an offended expression.

"I don't need looking after by you," he said. Seek craned his neck to look up at Terror and then nodded solemnly at Chase. "I'll take care of him."

Chase set off, Shadow at her heels, doing his best to keep up. She wasn't sure what she was going to have to do to stop Grandmother, but she knew she would do whatever it took.

This is my last chance, and I won't let it go. Not this time.

CHAPTER TWENTY-TWO

"*Thank you, Spider,*" Bramble said. "*Whatever* happens now, I'm glad I'm still here to see it." His voice was still raspy and painful, but the pain wasn't so bad—it reminded him that he was really here, alive, when he so easily could have been lying dead at the bottom of the ravine. The snake had tightened around his neck, Moonflower had reached out her hands . . . and then his eyes had opened, and he'd been lying in the clearing, with Spider, Moth, Moonflower, and Prance looking down at him.

Spider patted his arm gently. "I know how you feel. Spider knows, don't worry about it."

Bramble's chest ached where the baboon had thumped on it, and his skin was bruised and scraped all around his neck and shoulders, but he was alive.

He looked up beyond the canopy of the tree where they were sheltering. The creatures in the clearing had hardly

taken their eyes off the sky since he'd woken up: baboons and
lions and Sky and Prance herself, mesmerized by the spreading black cloud that was starting to block out the sun. And
now, something was traveling on the wind. It rained down
into the clearing, scraps of black and gray ash that felt warm
when they landed on Bramble's skin.

The trees were full of birds, and though he couldn't speak
skytongue, it was clear they were worried. They were making
a racket up there, chattering away, while Prance tried to listen and talk to them. Every so often, a few would try to take
off, fly into the falling ash, and quickly hurry back to the tree
branches to huddle and shelter there instead.

"It's the mountain, isn't it?" Moonflower said. "Something's happened to the Spirit Mouth. I can feel it."

"There was a great fire in the mountains once before," Sky
muttered. "When Titan was defeated. There was so much
smoke and flame, the sky seemed like it was on fire. But
this . . . I've never seen anything like this."

Bramble shuddered. He didn't like the flicker of fear he
saw pass across the great elephant's face. If she was afraid,
what chance did the rest of them have?

Moonflower's hand found Bramble's, and she squeezed, a
little too hard.

"I'm right here," he said.

"Yes, but you *weren't*," she snapped. "You vanished, all on
your own. If I hadn't followed you, you'd be *dead*. So shut up."

Bramble turned away. She had every right to be angry. She
was right, of course she was. But it hurt, too. Yet again, he had

tried to help, and all he'd done was make things worse. What could he do to make it up to her, when the world seemed to be ending around them? What could he do about any of it?

More creatures had started arriving at the clearing, seeking out the new Great Mother for advice and guidance, and some of them seemed upset when she didn't have much to give them, but the eerie blanket of ash made all their grumbling feel muffled—at least until there was a crash of breaking branches and a large warthog burst into the clearing, panting and snorting.

"Great Mother!" she cried. She ran over to Prance, skidding to a halt in the ashy grass. "Come quick! Something's happening to the watering hole! It's . . . it's terrible!"

Prance nodded, and Bramble got to his feet, despite Moonflower clinging to his hand.

"I want to see it," he said. "Whatever it is."

"All right," she said, and they got up and followed Prance. Seemingly every other creature in the clearing had had the same thought, though she hadn't asked any of them to come with her—Prance walked ahead, surrounded by lions, with the warthog at her side, followed by the baboons and Sky, and trailed by a few of the largest, bravest birds who hopped from branch to branch to follow her through the trees. At the edge of the forest, a few of them settled on Sky's back, huddling close to her huge ears, and the elephant seemed happy to bring them along with her.

Eventually they all emerged from the forest and looked across the plain toward the watering hole, and Bramble caught his breath. The ash had been bad enough in the clearing, where at least some of it had been caught in the trees—out here in the open, it swirled through the air like pollen or falling leaves on a strong wind, settling over everything, giving the whole of Bravelands a dark and muted look.

Trying not to breathe in the ash, Bramble hurried along behind them toward the watering hole. Before they even reached it, it was clear something was wrong, even beyond the ash in the sky and the black cloud gradually blocking out the sun. The hippos were all out of the water, stomping around on the bank, grunting to one another. Chew was there too, sitting on a rock, his tail swishing. As they approached, Bramble realized that the air above the water wasn't quite the same as the air around it. The ash was behaving differently, swirling in strange directions. . . .

Moonflower gasped and gripped his arm again. "Bramble!" she said. "It's steaming!"

For a moment, Bramble simply didn't believe her. How could the watering hole be steaming? He had been immersed in that water not long ago, and it had been chilly even in the bright sunshine! And yet, when they walked a little closer, he saw that she was right—steam was rising from the surface of the water. Prance went up to the edge and put her nose down to sniff at it, then pulled away quickly. Behind her, Bramble saw that the water was bubbling and roiling.

"It's hot," Prance said. "Stay back, everyone! It's not safe."

"But how is this happening?" Moth asked, looking up at the sky. "Moonflower, didn't you say there was steam in the mountains? Moonflower?"

Bramble looked around and realized that his sister was frozen, staring into the steam. He and Moth, and a group of baboons and lions that had noticed Moonflower's strange expression, all stood by quietly and watched her.

"*Now?*" she said suddenly. Then she blinked and seemed to be back with them. She looked at Bramble and swallowed. "Um. Great Mother?" she called. Prance looked up and hurried over. The other animals parted to let her through.

"Moonflower—did you see something?" she asked.

"I heard the voice of the Great Spirit," Moonflower said, her voice slightly squeaky with disbelief. "I saw . . . so much. There was a leopard and her shadow crossing the plains, there was a river made of fire . . . and the Spirit told me that now is the time of Grandmother's greatest weakness. Now, while the sky is dark."

Bramble looked at Prance. Everybody did.

Prance bowed her head. She turned away, staring at the ground for a moment. Then she walked over to the jutting rock over the steaming water and clambered onto it.

"Everybody, listen," she called out. The creatures who'd followed her gathered around, and so did the hippos and Chew. Through the swirling ash, Bramble started to see other animals making their way toward her. "My friends," she said. "I have avoided conflict all my life. From the moment I was born, the Us guided me to run at the first sign of danger, like every gazelle must in order to survive. I am not a fighter. I have never even needed the Code—I have never had to kill to survive, unlike many of you. But then I lost the Us, and I lost my herd. At first, I felt desperate and alone. But being chosen by the Great Spirit, being blessed by Great Father Thorn . . . I realized something. I am not alone. I never have been. No creature can live completely alone, trusting only themselves. The great snake Grandmother *uses* other creatures, she infects them with her own mind. She doesn't have allies. She doesn't have friends. She just has . . . *thralls*. But we have allies and friends. We have each other."

"So what do we *do*?" asked the warthog.

"We do what our allies, the lions, would do," said Prance. "We don't run. We take the fight to Grandmother. Many have died already. More will die today. But it is time for us all to follow the Code. We will kill her, in order to survive."

There was a pause, and an intake of breath. Then Gallant stepped up beside Prance's rock, opened his jaws, and roared, a huge, angry roar that split the muted atmosphere. Sky raised her trunk in the air and trumpeted along with him. One by one, the animals at the watering hole joined the roar, the baboons hooting and slapping the ground, the hippos grunting.

Bramble and Moonflower looked at each other, took deep breaths, and bellowed, thumping their chests. Hope and energy flooded into Bramble as the sound of their war cry echoed across the plains.

CHAPTER TWENTY-THREE

Prance walked, her head held high, through the swirling ash and the growing darkness. She felt as if every step she took vibrated the ground beneath her hooves—perhaps because every step was matched by the paws and feet and hooves behind her.

When was the last time a gazelle led lions and gorillas into battle? she wondered. *I wish I could ask that other Great Parent gazelle—but I bet the answer is "Never"!*

It wasn't too terribly far along the river to the ravine, but it was far enough that she couldn't help thinking of Moonflower, who had followed her brother all the way there and then carried him all the way back. If there was ever an example of creatures working together, using their bonds of friendship to push them to great things, she couldn't think of a better one.

They met more animals along the way, too, and almost all of them joined the march. A wandering wolf followed them, and a herd of zebra. Prance broke away from the crowd to speak softly to a small family of dik-diks, and instructed them to run and find other creatures, bigger creatures, who wanted to join the fight.

"Prance!" called a voice, and Prance's heart skipped a beat. She recognized that voice. It was Shortsight, the giraffe. He had escaped Menacepride after all! She ran to him and then stopped, suddenly awkward as she realized that she had never gone back for him, that she should have sent Gallant, or done *something* more to help him.

But Shortsight didn't seem angry with her. He trotted over and bent his long neck to touch his nose to hers.

"I'm so happy to see you again," Shortsight said. "Everybody says you're our Great Mother now!" Prance looked around his shoulder and saw a herd of giraffes approaching them, seven or eight of the large creatures. "They found me after I escaped and let me join them," Shortsight said.

"I'm so pleased."

But there was no more time for reunions. There was another rumble from the sky, and Prance braced herself for the earthquake to follow—but this time, the animals all yelped and looked up at the sky as lightning crackled through the black cloud.

"We have to get to Grandmother before this gets worse," Prance said. "Is your herd with us?"

"Of course," said Shortsight. "We're with you, Great Mother."

They hurried on along the river, picking up a family of

buffalo and a troop of meerkats. But the more animals who joined her, the darker the storm overhead seemed to grow. The sun was long gone from the sky behind the black clouds, the ash underfoot making the smaller creatures choke as they walked. The lightning came faster and brighter as they approached the ravine. And then suddenly, Prance saw a flash of something else. An orange light—but it wasn't coming from the sky. In the hazy distance, something was happening to the mountain. Rivers of flame were beginning to run down its slopes, just like Mud and Moth's vision. They looked like huge, fiery snakes. Fire flickered through the jungle, leaving it dead and blackened. Every few moments, sparks and splashes of the burning liquid could be seen flying from the top of the mountain.

Prance wanted to cry out in horror.

All the creatures who had lived on the mountain. Would any of them survive? What would be left once Grandmother was done?

But she swallowed her pain and pressed on through the dark and the ash, until the forest that grew around the ravine was just ahead. Birds flocked around them, landing on the rocks by the river, but avoiding the branches of the trees—smoke curled between them, like gray snakes.

She paused a little way from the ravine and turned to look at her followers. There were so many now—and she had no idea if it would be enough.

"Gallant, Bramble," she said, as the lion and the young gorilla hurried to her side. "I'm going in to find out if I can see what Moonflower's vision meant about Grandmother being vulnerable. I'll be back in a moment. Stay vigilant."

"We will, Great Mother," said Gallant.

Prance didn't even sit down and get comfortable this time. She walked out of her body, pausing only briefly to look back and see it collapse softly to the ground behind her.

It was a relief to be able to walk among the trees and down into the ravine without having to breathe the smoky air, but everything else she saw beyond the lip of the ravine was eerie and frightening. The river was steaming, just like the watering hole, filling the valley with mist as well as drifting ash. Snakes dangled from every branch, just like Bramble had said. Their heads turned to watch as Prance passed, but they didn't move to try to attack. At the bottom of the ravine, she could sense the building heat even though her body was still outside in the storm.

The gorillas were awake, but they weren't moving. There was one perched on a rock by the hot stream, another one in a tree overhead, more of them standing on the bank.

"Turn back," they said in eerie unison, their voices echoing down the ravine.

Prance ignored them. Their eyes followed her as she moved between them, but they didn't reach for her or even turn their heads.

"Turn back," they said again. "Do not dare to disturb the Queen's slumber."

They can't stop me in this form, Prance thought. *They can only try to scare me.*

She weaved between the gorillas, trying to ignore their whispering.

"Turn back," they kept saying. "Or face your doom."

The clearing where she'd confronted Grandmother last night was full of steam and falling ash. Lying beneath a thick covering of the warm gray flakes was Grandmother herself. Prance tilted her head as she looked down. Underneath the ashes, the quality of Grandmother's skin had changed—it was translucent and milky, not like the vibrant black and red scales she'd seen last night.

Then Grandmother's eye opened, and her head turned a little, leaving the covering of skin where it was, her new skin moving underneath the old in a way that made Prance feel almost dizzy.

Have you come to watch, little mother? Grandmother said.

Prance took a step away. She should leave. This was what Moonflower's vision had meant. Grandmother was still shedding. She could hardly move. They needed to march on her, *now. . . .*

Please stay, if you like, said Grandmother. Her voice in Prance's head was weak, but still somehow infinitely smug. *Witness my final rebirth. Soon my skin will be as tough as stone. And it won't just be this world I'll rule over.*

"What do you mean?" Prance asked. *Tell me,* she thought. *Tell me everything. . . .*

When I take my final form, and the fire snakes pour from the mountain, the shadow realm itself will be within my grasp. You will have nowhere to flee to. Do you believe me? Perhaps you would like to see for yourself.

Grandmother's tongue flicked out of her mouth . . . and detached itself, dropping to the ashy ground as a wriggling black snake of shadow. Prance's shadow-self froze, locked up with horror just as her physical body would have, and before she could move the snake had wound around her leg. She tried to pull away, her back legs lifting from the ground, but she was stuck tight in the coil of the shadow-snake. Panicking, she kicked at it with her other hoof, but the snake had no real face to aim for—it was just a piece of Grandmother's spirit, peeled away to do battle with hers.

You put your faith in your shadow tricks, Grandmother said, and her real tongue flickered out and tasted the air. *But my spirit is just as powerful as yours, and there is no world where you can escape my coils. . . .*

CHAPTER TWENTY-FOUR

Shadow and Chase found the hyenas' prey, half of a zebra dangling from the crook of a tree in the shadow of another kopje, and Shadow tore into it. After that they ran together, the speed and power returning to Shadow's limbs.

They followed the trail of the gorillas, easy enough even normally with the smashed undergrowth and trampled grass, but now they had the path they'd trodden through the ash to follow too. It fell around them in swirling gusts, glowing embers fizzling out in drifts against the rocks and the trunks of trees. Shadow's pelt was soon more gray than black, and they both had to stop to clean their faces and paw at their eyes more than once.

"Chase, look," Shadow said, when they'd stopped for her to try to spit out a piece of ash that had landed on her tongue. She turned and saw the fire snakes. They were spilling down the mountain, just like Grandmother had said. How long until they got to the plains? What would happen when they did?

"We have to go," she coughed.

They caught up with the gorillas just as they were slipping into a forest on the horizon. With the creatures out of view, Chase and Shadow put on a burst of speed, and they reached the edge of the trees in a few moments. Chase bunched her muscles to leap over the roots and into the forest beyond—but there *was* no forest beyond. She skidded to a stop, looking down, her breath catching. The trees were growing along and over the edge of a steep cliff. The valley below was full of mist and ash.

"They went down there?" Shadow asked, panting.

"Looks like it. Come on," Chase said. "It's no more difficult than some parts of the mountain. Look, there are trees to jump to almost all the way down."

"I avoided those parts of the mountain," Shadow muttered. But he followed her into the ravine.

It was dark under the trees, even darker than the plains under the black-smoke storm cloud. The mist was just water; it left her fur damp and her eyes watering as she jumped from one slippery moss-covered rock and tree branch to the next. But the scent was strange. It was the same acrid scent she'd smelled in the caves of the spirit vent, before she and Grandmother had left the mountain. Something of the mountain was here now. . . .

"Chase!" Shadow hissed. He padded along the branch beside her and pointed down with his nose. "Look."

Down below there was a thin trickling stream, giving off wisps of mist, and beside it stood a pair of gorillas. They were looking up at the top of the ravine, but they didn't seem to have noticed the two leopards. They didn't move. They didn't blink, despite the swirling steam right in front of their faces. Chase wasn't even sure they were breathing.

"Are they guarding something?" Shadow whispered.

"Grandmother," said Chase. "I have to get past them."

"There'll be more," Shadow warned.

"I know. But I came this far, and there's not much time. Don't worry. I've had a lot of practice at avoiding gorillas." She licked his ear, then turned around and set her eyes on the next branch along.

"Go." Shadow nudged her forward, and together they jumped, landing softly, hardly stirring the leaves around them.

He was right. There were more gorillas. Chase pressed slowly on, paw over paw, her belly low to the trees and the rocks. Shadow walked in her pawsteps, letting her navigate the path through the trees. The gorillas' gazes were fixed, and she could avoid them if she was careful. She still almost gave them away as she slunk around behind a tree trunk and nearly stepped on a brown snake. It reared up and hissed at her, and, swallowing a panicked yowl, she grabbed it in her jaws and threw it as hard as she could into the empty air. It dropped, landing in the undergrowth beside one of the gorillas, which slowly bent over to look at what had fallen. Chase took the opportunity to slip past with Shadow, keeping her eyes on the branches for more snakes. There were plenty, but she could avoid them too, as long as she was careful. . . .

Then there was a distant roar of earth cracking and trees shaking.

"Hold on!" Chase hissed, flattening herself to the tree branch she was on and gripping it with her claws. But Shadow was mid-jump, and as he landed the tree they were in began to shake itself, back and forth, as if it was trying to throw him off. His back paws slipped, and he let out an involuntary yelp and caught himself by the claws on the tree bark, dangling over a sheer drop with his back legs and his tail.

Down below, the gorillas' faces turned in a single, eerie motion, and they looked right at Shadow. Howls of rage echoed through the ravine, the thumping rhythm of hundreds of gorillas pounding on their broad chests, and the crashing of fern and branch as they sprang up into the trees.

"Go!" Shadow yelled, but Chase couldn't just leave him— she ran to him, leaned dangerously far over the branch, and grabbed the scruff of his neck, dragging him back up onto the perch.

"Come on!" she gasped, and turned tail to run. Thick fingers were already pulling down on the branches of the tree they stood in, and hissing snakes were waking up and swarming over the next to intercept them. She sprang, turned, waited for Shadow to jump too, and then they hurtled together through the branches. If they could just get out of the gorillas' sight, then maybe . . .

Suddenly, a bird passed over Chase's head, and she startled and crouched low to the rock she was standing on. But when she looked up, there was nothing there . . . except a shadow that moved overhead, not bird-shaped, but strangely birdlike nevertheless. It moved across the canopy, and Chase followed it almost without thinking. It led her to a high branch sticking out into misty, ashy nothingness, and vanished into the swirling air.

Chase looked back, and she didn't see the gorillas—but she didn't see Shadow, either. She shivered and peered down into the clearing.

Grandmother was right below her, her huge coils resting in a strangely still heap.

Hope and fear rose into Chase's throat all at once. Grandmother was shedding, but she was still encased within her old skin. Maybe it wasn't too late.

She saw the shadow again, passing over Grandmother's still face. Except it wasn't quite the same. Chase squinted, blinked, and tried to wash her eyes, afraid that the ash had gotten into them and she couldn't trust her own vision. Grandmother's head was lying where it had been, moving just a little, but definitely still inside the thick, peeling skin. And yet Chase could *also* see her tongue flicking out, licking around another dark shape. A struggle, as if Grandmother was tethering something, stopping it from flying away.

She didn't know what was happening, but she knew one thing: Grandmother was not looking at her.

She sprang, claws out, teeth bared. Grandmother's one working eye looked up, saw Chase, and narrowed in fury just before she landed on the back of the snake and buried her teeth in her neck, tearing through the delicate discarded skin and into the soft, new scales beneath.

Grandmother screamed, a hoarse hissing sound that hurt Chase's ears, and reared up, bursting through the fragile skin. Chase held on with every ounce of strength she had left as the surface she was standing on suddenly turned vertical. The scales were strangely slippery, and a few of them peeled off under her claws as she tried to keep her grip, fluttering to the ground to lie among the ashes.

Grandmother swung her neck from side to side, and Chase hung on, locking her jaw and raking her claws over the snake's skin, though the world around her shook and swayed and flipped upside down. Grandmother jerked and groaned and flopped forward for a moment. Chase tore her jaws free, a mouthful of cool black snake blood dripping down over her muzzle, and began to climb up the snake's back, clawing every inch of the snake that she could reach, blindly attacking until suddenly Grandmother threw herself to the ground, and with a horrible jolt that rattled the teeth in Chase's head she was thrown off the snake's neck, rolling in the ash and landing in the hot water of the stream.

Chase scrambled to her paws and faced Grandmother head-on. Grandmother raised herself up slowly, tearing free of the old skin, her face turned to the sky. When the snake looked down again, Chase saw what she had done: Grandmother's last good eye was gouged across, bleeding and half-closed. Her head swayed, her tongue flicking out to taste the air.

Do you think you've won? I can hear you breathing, Chase, she said, in a high, hysterical voice that vibrated between Chase's ears and made her cringe and back away. *I can smell you. I don't need eyes to destroy your kind. I have a thousand eyes. I see your mate, the black leopard. He thinks he's going to save you. I see your allies climbing down the waterfall, and I will see them fall under the fists of my gorillas. All Bravelands will be mine! Your cub will die, and you will live to see it, I promise you!*

"Chase!" Shadow burst from the undergrowth. "They're coming, I couldn't lose them. . . ."

"Shadow, keep back!" Chase yelled, running to put her body between him and Grandmother. She saw his yellow eyes go wide with terror—but by the time she had turned back to face the giant snake, she was gone from the clearing, leaving her old skin gently settling to the ground.

CHAPTER TWENTY-FIVE

The ground shook, and the animals gathered around Prance's prone body let out yelps and cries of fright as a great noise rose from the ravine: the roaring and thumping of gorillas about to attack.

Between Sky's forelegs, Prance's body twitched and shuddered, and not because of the shaking ground. A deep red stain appeared at the corner of her mouth, and a trickle of blood ran down her muzzle and dripped into the grass.

"Great Mother!" Sky cried, and she tried to gently shake Prance awake—but she didn't stir except to let out a weak moan and toss her head back.

"What's happening to her?" Moth gasped.

Bramble looked at Gallant.

"We have to go down there," he said.

"The gorillas and the baboons and some of the preda-tors can get down the waterfall rocks, the way I did before," Moonflower put in. "I can show the way."

"Good," said Gallant. "I'll send my pride to find any way they can. The zebras and giraffes can watch the top of the ravine. Sky and I will guard the Great Mother."

"With our lives," said the elephant, standing over Prance's small body. "The hippos won't be much good on a cliff either. They can stay with me."

"Let's go," said Bramble.

Moonflower frowned at him. "How's your chest?" she said.

"Good enough," Bramble snapped.

Moonflower nodded. "Then follow me."

She turned and began to run for the ravine, following the path of the steaming river. Bramble fell in behind her, trying not to pant too hard as he ran. His throat still hurt, much more than he was willing to let on. But he pushed through, thinking of Prance, her spirit maybe trapped or hurt in there without their help.

I can't stay behind, he thought. *I won't sit here useless while everyone else fights to save Bravelands!*

Moth, Bug, Cricket, and the rest of the baboons were right behind him, the lone wolf flanking to their right, the lions spreading out along the ridge to start to clamber down between the trees. Moonflower stepped right to the edge and then reeled back, gasping. The mist of the waterfall was ris-ing faster, and when Bramble leaned over to see he realized the stones beneath his hands were warm, almost too warm to touch.

They clambered down in silence, following Moonflower's path between the slippery rocks, avoiding the splashes of water from the steaming waterfall.

They got to the bottom of the ravine and started to make their way through the ferns and the rocks. Bramble walked along the ground, Moonflower and the wolf beside him, while the baboons took to the trees and flanked them on either side. He scanned every tree trunk, every stone, prepared to come across the gorillas at any moment. But whatever they had been screaming about, it seemed to have led them away from the waterfall. There were still snakes draped all around, but the wolf and the baboons were stalking them, and with many creatures watching out for them they were much easier to avoid.

There was still roaring in the distance, the occasional thump of gorilla fists, and through the thick mist Bramble heard the yowl of a big cat and a scream he couldn't identify. But all of it felt strangely far-off and muted.

Suddenly, he stepped over a log and found himself looking at a part of the ravine that felt distinctly different. The stream trickled through broken branches and shriveled ferns, between tree trunks stripped of their leaves. It seemed as if this whole place had suddenly died, infected by disease.

What did this? Could trees be infected with the sandtongue curse?

He looked up at the trees and saw baboons gingerly poking their heads from the thicker canopy, looking for a way across. A few of them started to clamber along the rocks at the side of the ravine. Bramble took a deep, shaky breath and knuckled just a few steps out into the terrible broken undergrowth.

"This is a place of death," Moonflower whispered behind him.

"We have to get through," Bramble muttered back. "We have to find Great Moth—"

He cut off with a yelp as a scream echoed through the empty space, and a wild, screeching swarm of creatures burst from the forest all around him. Vervet monkeys, blue monkeys, olive baboons, and even a troop of tiny galagos with their large, liquid eyes and giant ears. All of them drooling and spitting, wild-eyed, hurling themselves into the trees, grabbing and biting at the baboons. All at once, the trees over Bramble's head became a battlefield, leaves and ash falling around him as the screaming of the infected and the shocked roars of the baboons shook the branches.

A pair of vervet monkeys sprang up from beneath a pile of twisted ferns and grabbed on to Bramble's arms, trying to bite at his neck. He roared and threw himself bodily at the nearest tree, squashing one of them between him and the trunk. Its grip failed and it fell to the ground, stunned, but the second got its teeth into Bramble's shoulder, until Moonflower pulled it free and tossed it across the clearing and into the trunk of another tree.

"Run!" Moth yelled. Bramble looked up and saw her swinging from one arm with a blue monkey dangling from her legs. She kicked at it, hard, and it lost its grip and fell. "You two, run! We've got this!" she cried.

"Come on," Moonflower said. She grabbed a fallen branch and broke into a run, swinging it at a galago that stood in her way. Bramble ran with her. They had to get to Grandmother! They charged across the dead space, flinching away from dripping, moldy branches. The terrible feeling lasted only a few elephant-lengths, and then they were hurtling into the lush green forest once more, leaping over logs and splashing in the hot stream.

Suddenly, Moonflower fell. Her legs were tangled in the coils of a snake, and Bramble saw her reach for him and felt a sense of awful familiarity. He tried to grab for her hands, as she'd grabbed him when he'd been entangled in the snakes, but she was being dragged backward, and his hands missed hers by a hair.

Strong, black-haired arms grabbed on to him, pulling him away. The gorillas!

He squirmed and scrambled against them, but they seemed as immovable as stones.

"Moonflower!" he yelled.

"Bramble!" she replied. "You gorillas, let him go! He's one of you!"

But he wasn't, not anymore. The gorillas grabbed his arms and legs and carried him bodily over the forest floor, then heaved and threw him ahead of them to land on his back in the hot water, the wind escaping his lungs in a strangled groan.

It wouldn't come back. He couldn't breathe. He clawed at his neck, thinking another snake was crushing his throat, but there was nothing there. He choked in a breath at last, his limbs going limp, staring up at the canopy above him that seemed to swirl over his head. Mist and ash rained down on him as he gasped for air.

But no fists did. There were no thrown sticks or kicks to his sides. For a moment, unable to see the other gorillas, he felt as if he'd been hurled out of the world he knew and into another forest, where he was completely alone.

Then he managed to roll over in the water and sit up, and he saw that he wasn't alone at all. Instead, he was surrounded. Gorillas were standing in a circle all around him, as still as rocks, watching him. Goldbacks and Blackbacks, a Silverback he recognized from another troop, even a young Blackback who couldn't be more than a year old. And every one of them had a snake. Most of them draped theirs over their shoulders; some wore them curled around their wrists or their necks.

They began to huff and grunt, thumping their chests in rhythm, and then stepped toward him slowly, looking at Bramble as if they wanted nothing more than to tear him limb from limb. He got to his feet and grabbed a stone from the streambed, but he didn't throw it.

He knew it wouldn't make any difference. Either his allies

would come, or he was facing his death. . . .

The gorillas changed what they were doing—not crowding into their circle, but opening it at one end, so that suddenly he was trapped between two long lines of gorillas. One of them seized and pushed him to the next in the line, and he found himself shoved and twirled between them, the snakes hissing at him as he went. He tried to shoulder his way between two gorillas and out of the line, but their snakes snapped and bared their teeth, and he recoiled.

I can't get bitten now! If I'm about to die, I'll die with my own mind!

At last he was shoved forward into an empty space and fell to his knees, dizzy and bruised, in front of Burbark Silverback.

Burbark stood at the top of another waterfall, where the stream fell away in steps into a deeper part of the ravine. Bramble could hear snarling and hissing down beyond the drop—it was hard to make out through the mist, but he thought he could see movement.

Great Mother? Is that you?

He looked up slowly at his father's face. Burbark's hollow cheeks and his deep-set eyes made his face look like a skull draped in loose skin. He had a snake too, a small, bright green one that slithered over his shoulders and whispered in his ear.

"Why have you come?" Burbark said, in a voice as low as the rumbling of the earth.

"To help the Great Mother," Bramble answered. "To kill Grandmother."

"You seek death," said Burbark. He turned his face to

the sky, and his snake crawled around his neck and bit him, digging its fangs in deep. Burbark shivered and gasped in a contented sigh. Bramble's stomach turned over, disgust and grief filling his heart, and he sprang up from his knees and made a grab for the snake.

Burbark's hand came up, as fast as the striking snakes, and seized Bramble's wrist.

"You seek death," he said again. "And you have found it."

He took the snake from his own neck, let it drop gently to the ground, and then pulled back his fist. Bramble ducked and charged, trying to bowl his father over, but even wasting away, Burbark was too strong, and he stood his ground and twisted Bramble's arm. Burning pain seared around Bramble's wrist, and he yelled out and dropped back to his knees.

In a flash, Bramble's memory showed him a picture he hadn't thought about in what felt like a long time: Burbark playing in the ferns with him when he was just a baby, picking him up and throwing him with infinite gentleness, letting Bramble chew on his fingers, bowling himself over in soft moss and letting Bramble sit on his chest, declaring Bramble the winner of the fight.

And then another: the gorilla troop, before they were cursed, standing around the broken body of his brother, Cassava.

The sandtongue Burbark had already murdered one of his sons for challenging Grandmother's plans. He wouldn't hesitate to do it again.

And the Burbark that Bramble remembered would hate himself for it.

Bramble let out a roar and used Burbark's grip on his arm to yank him off his feet. Burbark's grasp failed as he fell, eyes wide with surprise. He reared up a second later and tried to thump Bramble on the side of the head, but Bramble ducked under his arm and came up beneath his shoulder, throwing him down onto his side. With a roar of anguish, Bramble brought his fists down on his father's chest. Burbark yelled in pain, but he still managed to shove Bramble away, limp to his feet, and lock his arms around his neck.

They grappled with each other, splashing and slipping in the water. Burbark's fingers found Bramble's face and clawed for his eyes, but Bramble threw himself into a headbutt, pushing the hand away and smacking into Burbark's mouth with a *crunch*. Burbark spat out a bloody tooth and roared with rage, shoving back at Bramble. . . .

Bramble's feet met empty air. For a moment, Burbark's own feet skidded on slippery rock, and then the ravine turned upside down as they both tumbled over the edge of the waterfall. Rocks smacked into Bramble's back and Burbark's shoulders as they rolled over and over, hot water splashing into their eyes. Bramble could only hold on to Burbark and yell his pain to the sky as he felt his skin catch and tear on the loose stones. They fell once, twice, and then a third time, down into a shallow pool. Bramble landed on his side in the water. He shoved Burbark away from him and tried to push himself up, but his wrist screamed in agony and he almost blacked out.

He lay in the steaming pool, his breath rasping, waiting for Burbark to get back to his feet and attack again.

But there was no movement, and no sound from his father except for a thin, weak, rasping breath.

"Burbark," Bramble gasped, scooting closer, cradling his arm against his chest. He looked down, his vision pulsing with the pain, and saw that the water was beginning to flow red around Burbark's shoulders. His head had hit a rock that sat just below the surface.

His eyes were open, but Bramble didn't think he was seeing anything.

"Oh, Father . . . ," he groaned. "No, I didn't . . . I didn't want this, I didn't . . ."

He could hear shouts and thumps from up above, and then Valor's voice roaring commands. One of the gorillas was peering over the waterfall, and then looking down the ravine . . . but it wasn't one of their troop. It was Moonflower.

She clambered down to him.

"Father," she whispered, lowering herself into the water beside Bramble.

She took a moment, staring at Burbark. Bramble wondered if she was feeling what he was feeling: hollow.

Then she grabbed Bramble's shoulder.

"We have to go," she said.

"He's still alive," Bramble heard himself say, though the words seemed to almost come out of the air around him. "I can't leave him like this."

"We *have to*," Moonflower said. "Don't you feel it?" She

pointed, deeper into the ravine.

There was light shining through the trees. In the mist and the ash, for a moment it almost looked beautiful. Then Bramble realized what it was. A wild orange glow, heralded by black smoke and spitting fire.

The liquid fire from the mountain. It was here.

CHAPTER TWENTY-SIX

Prance woke up with a jolt like a lightning strike, rolled to her hooves, and then staggered against Sky's tree-trunk-like legs. She could taste blood, and her eyes were watering.

"Great Mother!" Sky said, bending down to speak softly to her. "Are you all right?"

"Grandmother . . . the leopard . . ." Prance leaned against Sky's leg and tried to clear her head. "Chase saved me!"

"Prance," said Sky. "Bramble and the others went in after you, but—"

She looked up suddenly, drawing herself up to her full height. One of the giraffes let out a yelp of fright.

"What? What do you see?" Sky staggered out a few steps, her knees weak, and followed the gaze of the taller animals, until she saw what they were staring at and her pelt twitched with dread.

A burst of liquid fire rose from the rocks in the distance, and a plume of smoke.

"No," Prance gasped. "It's so close. . . ."

"It's flowing like a river," the giraffe cried. "It's filling the riverbeds, the valleys . . . it's coming so fast!"

"That fire's going to flow right down into the valley," Prance said. "Bramble and the others will be burned up!"

And the gorillas too, she thought. *And hundreds and hundreds of snakes . . . Grandmother doesn't care for anyone but herself.*

"What about Grandmother?" asked Mud.

"I don't think she's still there," Prance said. "These are her fires, she knew this was coming all along."

Prance felt the panic rising in the crowd of animals as they saw the fire spreading over the plains. The ground shook as many of them turned to flee, and the air resounded with the worried cries of the rest. Prance turned on them.

"Run," she told them. "Get away from here, go!"

"You have to run too," said Gallant.

"I can't just leave," Prance gasped. "What about the others? I won't just give up!"

"You can't help them if you're dead!" Gallant growled, and gently but bodily shouldered her out from between Sky's feet. She broke into a run, and they both sprinted away from the billowing smoke.

The whole plain was aflame. More and more creatures charged past them, animals that hadn't joined Prance's army bursting from their burrows and down from their trees.

Somewhere behind them, there was a bang and a sizzling sound, and Prance looked around in time to see liquid fire flowing into a watering hole, which exploded, sending burning orange droplets soaring into the air.

"Watch out!" Gallant said and nudged her out of the way. Prance staggered and then looked back when she heard Gallant cry out in pain. One of the drops had hit him on the side of the flank—it couldn't have been larger than a berry, but Gallant's fur was burning, giving out an awful smell, and he was limping with agony.

Prance turned back to try to help him, but between them one of the cracks in the dry earth suddenly began spouting steam, and a sense as strong as the Us itself grabbed her by the heart and told her to *run*. Sure enough, she backed away and turned to sprint for her life, and the gout of fire that burst out from the crack a few seconds later still spattered down around her. A single droplet struck her horn, and she yelled and tossed her head as flames sprang up and died.

"Gallant!" she yelled, turning to look back. But there was so much smoke now, rolling across the plains in huge clouds that almost seemed like creatures themselves. She couldn't see him. She couldn't even see the fire, only the painful orange glow.

Screams and roars and trampling hooves echoed all around her. Panic that gripped the plains. She hadn't traveled far from where she began, but suddenly she was lost, and all alone.

Which way should she go? Was there any way to reach

Gallant, or to get to the ravine and help the others? What could she even do if she did?

She started walking across the hot earth, through veils of smoke. She was afraid to even run, knowing she might come across yet more fire bursting through the ground.

More and more cracks in the earth were opening, glowing and spewing out smoke and ash. The air was boiling and choked with burning embers, and Prance was already panting. Her mouth was dry. The light of the sun was gone, except for a few weak rays that pierced the gloom, but there was light enough to see by—it was orange and dreadful, emanating from the burning rivers.

Prance thought of the tunnels beneath Bravelands, the ones that had carried water, and later Grandmother, all the way from the mountain. The threat had been under her hooves all this time, but she hadn't ever imagined it would be like this. . . .

Prance, said Grandmother's voice.

Prance stopped walking. The voice seemed to come from all around her, echoing inside her mind as if Grandmother had shed her body altogether and taken the form of one of the great rolling clouds.

How do you like my new realm, my dear? Grandmother said. *Do you see now? You thought you were special. That the Great Spirit spared you when you escaped your fate. Shadowless. Herdless. It has all brought you here. To die in my coils!*

Black smoke gave way to black scales, and Prance brayed

and reared up as Grandmother slithered out of the darkness.

Prance just had time to see that both her eyes were filmed over now: one was still dripping blood onto the sizzling ground. But she didn't seem to need her eyes to sense Prance's presence: her tongue flickered out, tasting the burning air, and before Prance could get out of the way Grandmother's jaws opened wide and snapped down hard on Prance's front leg.

Prance screamed as the pain tore through her, leaving her bloodied and gasping, her head spinning.

But right behind the pain, following like a lion giving chase to a herd of gazelle, was rage. She reared up and kicked out with her other hoof, again and again, battering the top of Grandmother's head. The snake flinched. Prance pressed her hoof to Grandmother's scales and pushed so hard she felt the blood begin to run in her throat again, as if a cut she didn't know she had had been torn open. At last, Prance managed to wrench her leg free. Blood coursed down it to the ground, but she couldn't feel the pain she knew she should be feeling. She took a wild swing at Grandmother's face with her hooves and then danced away, her injured hoof dangling in front of her. She turned and ran, limping but still fast, terrified that she would catch her other front hoof on something or run straight into the fire. Indeed, there was a burning rivulet right ahead of her, only about as wide as her. . . .

Let's see, she thought. She put on a burst of speed, going as fast as she could on three legs, and pushed herself into a leap across the top of the river. It was so hot she felt the hairs on the underside of her belly shriveling up, but she touched down safely on the other side and turned back to watch.

Grandmother pushed through the smoke.

I hear you, she said. *You can't escape me now.*

Her belly scales flopped down into the burning river . . . and she barely reacted at all. There was a sizzling sound and smoke rose, stinking of burning flesh, but the snake didn't recoil or even hiss.

Foolish little mother, Grandmother said. *I feel no pain. I cannot die!*

Prance turned again, pelting over the burning plain, steering hard away from a flaming tree that loomed out of the smoke suddenly, around rocks that seethed with heat. The smoke parted and she saw, in the direction she was running, a small herd of terrified zebra standing on an island of rock. Prance steered away from them. If it was the last thing she did, she would protect the creatures of Bravelands. . . .

But then she came to a cliff. The edge of a wide ravine, not the forested one where Grandmother had been hiding, but one that had been an empty valley of rocks and dust. It wasn't empty anymore. Down below, fire flowed, four or five elephants wide, black crust forming and breaking up as she watched.

Prance turned around, tried to go back, but Grandmother was right there. Prance saw her through the smoke just in time and ducked aside, letting her bad leg give way beneath her to dodge being caught in Grandmother's jaws again. The snake raised its head and swayed blindly around above her, sniffing, listening.

Prance went still. She tried not to even breathe, as Grand-mother's underbelly passed by her face. Perhaps she could still get out of this. . . .

But then she saw the state of the scales on the snake's belly. They were peeling, burned, awful-looking. The skin beneath looked raw and fleshy and vulnerable.

Chase did it, Prance thought. *She interrupted the final shedding. Grandmother doesn't feel pain—so she doesn't know that she'll burn, like any other animal.*

Prance thought about Runningherd. She thought about Bramble and Gallant, about Moth and Mud and Moonflower, about Sky. About Great Father Thorn. She felt his reassuring touch on her chest one more time.

I can taste your fear, Grandmother sneered, lowering her head right beside Prance.

With a cry, Prance tossed her horns again, spearing them into Grandmother's chin—they didn't penetrate the scales, but she didn't need them to. She just needed to annoy her.

Grandmother hissed.

"You'll never win!" Prance yelled. Grandmother swayed and snapped, but Prance hobbled back, out of reach, toward the edge of the ravine. "I am Prance Herdless," she said. "My own shadow couldn't catch me, and you won't either!"

She threw herself around, her hooves slipping on the ash, and sprinted as hard as she could for the ravine. Faster, faster, until she saw the drop into bright fire open below her. With Grandmother's heavy slithering and cold breath right behind her, feeling the hot air stir as the snake tried to snap at her tail, Prance struck her hooves down on the rock, tensed every sinew in her body, and sprang out over the edge.

The next moment seemed to stretch on forever, Prance's body hanging in the air, almost as if she was flying across the ravine in her shadow-form. But the scent of burning fur was real, the searing heat was real. And a moment later, so was the sound of Grandmother grunting as she threw herself out over the ravine, and the sickening *crunch* of breaking bones as she snapped her jaws down on Prance's hindquarters. Light filled Prance's vision as they plummeted together to the fiery surface of the burning river.

Prance squeezed her eyes closed and let herself float from her body, her shadow streaming out and away from the ravine. She landed on the opposite side and turned, her shadow-legs twitching as she could still faintly feel the sensation of Grandmother's fangs sunk deep in her flank.

Below her, in the burning river, Grandmother's full body was thrashing and convulsing as it sank slowly beneath the surface. The great snake might feel no pain, but she knew now that the fire was consuming her, and her scream of panic and of fury echoed across the plains, before it was cut off as the molten rock swallowed her up.

Prance caught a final glimpse of her own body, broken-backed and limp, her horns blazing from her head as if they were made of pure white fire, before she too sank and was lost.

All the pain ended. Prance's shadow-body felt strong and cool again, as she stood alone on the cliff, the smoke swirling around her.

I died, she thought. *But I'm still here.*

What happens now?

CHAPTER TWENTY-SEVEN

"I have him," Bramble said, bracing with his good arm on the rocks at the top of the ravine, with Burbark lying limp against his shoulder.

Moonflower threw herself up and over the edge, then leaned down to grab Burbark and drag him after her. Bramble climbed up last, gasping, his wrist searing with pain.

Behind them, the whole ravine was ablaze. When the liquid fire had met the boiling stream, the explosion had been immense. Now every tree and fern that wasn't completely subsumed by the horrible burning rock was catching fire.

In front of them, there was a motley crowd of animals—all those who had made it out of the ravine so far. They paced and panicked, some of them running off into the smoke, others lying down and pressing themselves to the ground in terror.

"Can't stay here," Moonflower said. "Got to get some distance from the trees."

She hefted Burbark over her shoulders once again and helped Bramble to his feet. They stumbled a little way away, until they could no longer see the flames from the ravine through the black clouds around them. The smoke cleared to show a rock formation, miraculously not falling into fire, and Moonflower staggered over to it and laid Burbark down, gently, with his back to the warm stones.

Blood caked his back and shoulders, turning the silver hair a deep red. His head fell back, and Bramble collapsed to sit on the ground beside him.

"He's still breathing," Moonflower said, holding her hand in front of their father's open mouth. "A little."

"Is . . . is there something we can do?" Bramble asked. "Could we try Spider's trick?"

"I don't know if—"

There was a sound of soft footsteps, and Moonflower looked up and then turned suddenly, pressing her back to the rocks.

"Don't come any closer!" she gasped.

Through the swirl of smoke, gorillas were knuckling toward them. But something was different. Bramble stared, trying to understand, until finally the smoke cleared a little more, and he saw the face of Apple Goldback.

Deep confusion creased her brow, and her walking faltered as Moonflower shouted out. She put up a hand, stared at it, and then dropped it again.

"Moonflower?" she said weakly. "What's happening? Where are we?"

Bramble realized what had seemed different about the gorillas. They were all wandering in different directions, stopping and starting, clutching burned limbs and looking around at the smoke with terror in their eyes. The calm, eerie unison of creatures being driven by something inside their heads was gone.

"The sandtongue curse," Moonflower gasped. "It's . . . it's broken!"

"What does that mean?" Bramble asked. "Is she . . ."

"B-bramble . . . ?"

Bramble turned. Burbark's eyes flickered open.

"Is that you?" he grunted.

"Father?" Bramble reached for Burbark's hand and found it limp and cool.

"What's happening?" Burbark tried to sit up, but then tensed with pain.

"Don't move," Moonflower said, hurrying to his other side, taking his other hand. "You're badly hurt!"

"How . . . how did . . . What is . . . ," Burbark slurred.

He turned his head, his eyes fixing on Bramble. They were unfocused and full of pain, but for the first time in many moons Bramble knew that his father was really looking out of them.

"There was . . . an accident," Bramble said. "You hit your head." Guilt was filling his heart, a wrenching, awful knowledge that if he had just held on a little longer, if he hadn't fought Burbark, if they hadn't fallen together, then his father could be standing here just like the other gorillas who were gathering around, whispering to one another in shock and confusion.

Burbark tried to clear his throat, then choked and tensed again.

"Can't . . . breathe properly," he said. "Think . . . I'm dying. Bramble. Where . . . where is Cassava?"

Moonflower covered her mouth with one hand. Bramble blinked to clear the smoke and the pain from his eyes. He should be honest. Right? He wasn't sure. Wouldn't Burbark want to know what had happened to his son?

"Father . . . ," he began. "Cassava is . . ."

"On his way," said Moonflower. Bramble looked up at her, and she nodded at him, and he felt a flush of relief. "You'll see him soon."

"Hmm. Need to talk to him. Need to tell him . . ." Burbark winced once more and clutched weakly at Bramble's hand. "You . . . are bigger," he said. "You've grown. So strong. Your mother would be proud."

He let go of Bramble's hand and reached up, though it seemed to cost him a great deal. He touched his fingertips to Bramble's forehead.

"You will make a fine Silverback one day," he said.

His hand slipped from Bramble's forehead and went limp. His eyes drifted shut, and the twitches and gasps of pain ended. Burbark's head fell against Bramble's shoulder, and the great Silverback slipped into Bramble's arms with something like a sigh.

Bramble let out a moan and gathered his father close, holding him tight.

There was a long pause. For a moment there was nothing but the crackling of flames, and the heavy, horrified breathing of the other gorillas. He looked up and saw that they had all fallen to their knees, holding themselves and one another.

"He wouldn't have wanted to know the truth," Moonflower muttered. "Not about Cassava, or . . . or any of it. His spirit will be with our ancestors, and he'll be at peace."

"Bramble," Apple said. She came forward, timidly, and put a gentle hand on Bramble's shoulder. "Please, tell us what happened. I . . . I don't remember much, but . . . Cassava's dead, isn't he?"

Bramble nodded.

Apple put both her hands down on the ground beside Bramble and bowed. One by one, the other gorillas copied her.

"Your hair *is* starting to go silver," Moonflower said, in an exhausted, almost amused tone. "I didn't tell you. I didn't want it to go to your head."

Bramble stared at her, and then at the others. He gently laid Burbark down on the ground and stood up, trying to clear his throat.

What could he possibly tell them?

"Something terrible happened to our troop," he said. "To almost all the mountain gorillas. To all of Bravelands." He swallowed and rubbed his hand over his face. The smoke was starting to lift, just a little, and he realized just how many gorillas had gathered around them. He could see several who had attacked him, who had tried to kill him. Even Apple. "You were cursed, but the curse has ended now. Nothing that happened until today was your fault, and from today, we have a chance for a fresh start. For all of us . . . who were lucky enough to survive."

Apple sat up and thumped her chest once, gazing up proudly at Bramble. He looked down at Moonflower, who gave a single nod.

The smoke rolled faster around them as the wind picked up, and a thin trail of sunlight fell over Burbark, casting a pooling shadow on the rock behind him, before the smoke rolled back, and the shadow faded away.

CHAPTER TWENTY-EIGHT

"Look out, there's another one here," Chase said. Shadow walked up behind her, treading lightly, following the trail she'd left in the ash and soot.

The fire snakes were still glowing in the ground, all across the plains. Almost all the smoke had cleared now, as the things that could burn had at last burned out. The smallest fissures were turning black, the fire snakes apparently slowing to a crawl and then to a seething stop—though they still burned so hot that Chase's whiskers curled when she looked at them. It hadn't been easy to find their way from the edge of the ravine where they had escaped to the Great Parent's forest.

Please, Great Spirit, let Seek and Terror have made it, Chase thought. *Please let Ribsnapper have got them here before the plains ripped themselves apart. . . .*

The forest itself, at least, seemed to have been far enough

from the mountain that it had escaped the worst of the fires. Creatures of all kinds were gathered under the unburned trees, zebras and cheetahs and crocodiles standing side by side and gazing out over the steaming red scars that covered the plains. They hardly blinked at the sight of the two leopards staggering into the shade of the trees.

It wasn't just the edge of the forest, either. There were animals everywhere. It seemed as if every creature that had been driven from its territory had headed straight here, perhaps hoping for the Great Mother's help, perhaps just running headlong away from the mountain. Their restless questions filled the air and followed the two leopards as they made their way through the forest: When would the watering hole fill again? How long would the steaming holes in the ground be too hot to approach? Would Bravelands always have these scars across its hide from now on?

"How long before we can go back to our burrow?" said a young meerkat to its mother.

"I think we'll have to make a new burrow," she replied.

At last, Chase poked her nose through the gap between two trees and looked into the Great Parent clearing. The ground here was ashy too, but it could hardly be seen between the baboons, lions, elephants . . . and hyenas. When Chase saw Ribsnapper, her heart raced and her ears pricked up. She ran into the clearing, leaping onto a tree stump, and there at Ribsnapper's paws was Seek.

"Seek!" she cried.

"Chase! Shadow!" Seek yowled and charged across the

clearing to scramble up onto the stump beside Chase and thrust the top of his head up under her chin. She licked and licked at him, and Shadow wound around them both.

"Chase?"

One of the baboons was making his way over to her, an elderly baboon with a sore-looking burn on the end of his tail.

"Are you the leopard who tried to kill the Great Mother?" he demanded.

"I'm so sorry," Chase said, hanging her head. "I didn't know. Grandmother threatened to kill my cub . . . but we'll go, if you want. I just came here to find him." She nuzzled Seek again.

"Let it go, Mud," said a younger female baboon. "Bramble said that she wasn't a bad leopard, and Grandmother's dead. Let's just let it go."

The younger baboon gave Chase a sad look, and now that Seek was pressed safely to her, Chase suddenly realized that the atmosphere in the clearing was . . . quiet.

"Where is the Great Mother now?" she asked. "I would like to offer my apologies."

The baboon shook her head. "We don't know. None of us know what happened. Grandmother was killed . . . but might have cost Prance her life."

"I'm so sorry," said Shadow.

Suddenly, a flash of golden-brown mane caught Chase's eye, and she gasped. "Look, it's Terror! He made it back too. Is . . . is that his father?"

She gazed at the large lion with the burn scar across his flank. Was that the same lion that had chased her halfway back to the mountains?

He chased me all the way to where his own lost son was hiding, she thought. *If that's not the Great Spirit at work, I'm not sure what is.*

The two lions were deep in conversation. Terror looked awkward, and Gallant seemed upset. But they were here, together, and they were talking.

"It'll be a long road for both of them," she said to Shadow. "After he spent so much time with Menace . . ."

But the Great Spirit will be with them, said a faint voice.

Chase startled and turned around, almost knocking Seek off the tree trunk. The voice . . . it didn't sound anything like Grandmother, but it felt like it had arrived in her mind the same way. Just like the vulture, up in the mountain. It was almost as if the infection had made a passage through her mind that could never be completely shut again. . . .

"Who said that?" asked Shadow.

There was nothing behind them, except for a motley collection of animals and dappled sunlight slipping through the trees above.

But all the animals were startling, looking around, as if they'd heard the voice too. The young baboon had turned to walk away, but now she froze and turned slowly, her eyes glittering.

"Prance?" she whispered. "Is that you?"

The old baboon beside her clutched at his heart. "What? Where?"

Moth, said the voice. *I'm here.*

The sunlight shifted, or rather the shadows did, flickering

across the ground in a way that didn't entirely make sense. Chase followed the dark patch with her eyes, then glanced up into the trees to see what could be causing it. The branches were still. And now she looked more closely at the shadow and saw it formed a familiar, impossible shape.

"Prance!" Moth scampered forward and raised her hands to the air where a creature would be standing, if the shadow belonged to a creature. . . .

It moved forward, and Chase gasped as she finally saw it clearly, cast against the side of one of the felled tree trunks: four straight legs, a long nose, and two graceful, pointed horns.

The gathered animals muttered and whispered to one another as the shadow of the Great Mother stood before them.

"It's Prance!" Moth's paws were shaking. "Everyone, it's Prance, she's alive!"

Moth, said the shadow of the Great Mother, in a tone that made Chase's fur prickle. *I'm sorry, but that's not true.*

Moth stared at Prance's shadow, and her expression fell. "Oh, Great Spirit . . . no . . ."

"But how can this be?" said Mud, hobbling over to the shadow.

My body is gone, said the Great Mother. *It's at the bottom of the burning river, with the body of Grandmother. But I wasn't in it when it burned up. I think . . . I think I'll be here until the Great Spirit chooses another host.*

"Do you know who it is?"

"Is the snake really gone?"

"Did it hurt?"

The gathered animals began to crowd around the shadow, asking questions, giving their condolences for Prance's death, and Chase slipped down from the tree trunk. She felt like an interloper here, among the creatures of the plains, at this vital moment for them all.

I don't know who the new Great Parent will be, Prance was saying. *I don't know how long I'll be with you.*

"It's so unfair!" Moth said, clasping her long fingers in front of her, a mixture of grief and joy crossing her face. "You were only Great Mother for a day or two!"

And in that time I destroyed Grandmother and saved Bravelands—with a lot of help from the rest of you, Prance's voice said. *I think I did all right.*

Chase slunk over to Ribsnapper.

"Well, isn't this something?" said the hyena, casting a wide and nonplussed stare at the baboon translating for the invisible gazelle. "The Great Devourer be praised, I suppose, for . . . whatever *this* is."

Chase pressed her head to the hyena's rough neck fur. "Thank you," she said. "For everything. We should go back to the mountain."

"Don't fall into the fire," said Ribsnapper. "And maybe I'll see you again one day."

Chase caught Terror's eye before she turned away. He nodded, an awkward, half-adult nod, and she returned it gracefully.

I exist in the world of shadows, Prance said to one of the elephants who had reached out its trunk to see if it could feel her presence. *Between our world and that of the spirits. You shouldn't be sad for me. When the Great Spirit first chose me—marked me, by separating my shadow from my body—I missed my herd, and I feared being alone. But now, I'm one with all of Bravelands! The poison of Grandmother is gone, and the mountain will go back to sleep in time. We all need time to recover. We need to forgive those who were infected. What's more, we need to show the sandtongues the care we'd show our grasstongue or skytongue siblings.*

There was a muttering among the animals—some approving, some a lot more doubtful. Chase sighed. She didn't envy Prance what she'd have to do now, until the next Great Parent was called. It would be hard enough to lead Bravelands if she had a body. . . .

"Come on," she said, turning back to Shadow. "It's a long walk back to the mountain. I don't even really know what's left when we get there, but I want to go and see."

"Me too," said Seek. "I want to see if our old den's still there!"

Chase doubted they were that lucky, but she remembered the meerkat mother they'd passed, and licked the top of Seek's head again.

"If it's not, we'll get to make a brand-new one," she said.

They reached the edge of the forest, walking against a tide of muttering animals who all seemed to have realized there was something very strange going on in the clearing. She put one paw out into the grass, and suddenly there was a whisper of wind across her back, and a voice spoke softly in her ear.

You saved Bravelands, Chase Born of Prowl, said the Great Mother. *And few creatures will ever know it. Thank you. Go home in peace, and good luck.*

They were making their way carefully between the steaming vents and dried-up riverbeds, about half a day later, when they crested the edge of a kopje and saw a host of black-furred gorillas moving across the plains. Chase froze, bracing herself to hide or run, when she realized that among the army— leading them—were two gorillas she recognized. Bramble and Moonflower were leading their families, all the gorillas who had marched from the mountain. With a few exceptions, that was. She scanned the crowd carefully, but there was no sign of Burbark Silverback.

She hung back nervously, not sure what the gorillas would do when they spotted the leopards. But Bramble's face lit up when one of the Goldbacks pointed out the small group, and he knuckled over to her with his sister at his heels.

"Chase! I'm glad you're alive—what happened to you?"

"Oh . . . I lived," Chase said. "We all lived."

Shadow and Seek were both standing behind Chase, peering over her shoulder at Bramble and the other gorillas behind him. She could sense their discomfort, and she couldn't blame them for it.

"How are . . . *they?*" Chase asked. She could make out the faces of gorillas she'd last seen speaking the words of Grandmother. There was even one eerily familiar face—the gorilla she'd fought at the watering hole, who had tried to murder

Seek. He was gazing at the leopards with no sign of recognition in his eyes at all.

"They don't remember anything," said Bramble. "Nothing from the first time they were bitten to the moment Grandmother died."

"*Oh.* Well . . . I'm glad for them," Chase said. *Does that mean that, of all the creatures Grandmother infected . . . I'm the only one who remembers her?*

There was an odd, horrible rightness in that.

"That must be what Prance meant when she talked about forgiveness," said Chase. "Do—do you know what happened to Great Mother?"

Bramble and Moonflower nodded.

"She came to us earlier," said Moonflower. "To say goodbye. It was strange, but I'm glad she survived. I mean . . . I'm glad she's still here," she added.

Chase nodded. "Me too. Are you going back to the mountain?" she asked.

"Yes," Bramble said. "But I don't feel like I'm running from the plains, like Kigelia was. I'm not afraid. I'm just . . . looking forward to going home."

"Also, he has to," said Moonflower. "Bramble Silverback has a troop to look after now."

Chase's eyes widened. "Bramble *Silverback*, huh?" she said. "So it's true this time?"

"More or less. I'm still getting used to it," said Bramble, with a shy smile. Then his brows shot up, as he seemed to have a thought. "Look—it's going to be dangerous on the mountain.

We don't know which parts will be safe. I don't want to be fighting you, as well as the fires. I don't want to fight you at all. Can we go back together? Divide the territory up fairly, like Great Mother would want us to?"

"I'd like that," said Chase. "And I think my mother and Cassava would both like that too."

There was some grumbling from the older gorillas when the three leopards joined their troop for the long walk back up the mountain, but a stern look from Bramble shut them up at once.

"I expect you'll want your own territory again," Shadow said, as they watched Seek scramble up over a rocky outcropping and peer up into the cloud-covered slopes. "I'll steer clear for a while, give you as much space as you need."

Despite everything, Chase suddenly felt strangely shy. "That's . . . really not necessary," she said. "You can stay. Just for a while. You know, for Seek's sake."

Shadow blinked, and his whiskers twitched into a pleased smile. "Oh," he said. "Well, if it's for Seek. We can stay together for a while."

He leaned his shoulder against Chase's, and side by side, flanked by the gorillas and with their eyes on the smoking mountain, they headed for home.

EPILOGUE

Stormrider wheeled over Bravelands, peering down at the cooling world beneath her. Red, burning fissures had gradually turned to searing coal, and then at last to little more than warm dirt and strange black rock. The first time the rains had come, it had been impossible to fly for all the steam, but now there were new watering holes, and fresh green growth was poking up through the ashy ground.

She whirled away to fly up over the foothills of the mountain and look down on the pool, the place she had always thought of as her home. Some of the new valleys that had formed when the fire snakes had flowed down the mountain slopes were now formed of shiny black glass, which glinted in the morning sunlight.

Stormrider rode the thermals down to perch on a branch above one of the glistening black streams, watched the water trickling peacefully below, and felt the weight of grief settle on her.

Bravelands was healing.

But Stormrider was all alone.

She hadn't found another living vulture since the great attack. Not one, in all of Bravelands. What would she do now? She would never have a mate, or young. She would never have anyone to pass on Windrider's stories to. Would all of vulture history die with her? And what about Bravelands? Who would taste the deaths of its creatures and help its new Great Parent, whoever it would be, if she was the only vulture left?

"It's too much," she muttered. "Windrider, I can't do it all on my own. What do I do?"

All is not lost, said a voice. Stormrider's feathers ruffled, and she let out a caw of surprise.

"Great Mother?" she said. "Is that you?"

Come with me, said the voice, and Stormrider looked down and saw a shadow far below her, almost the shape of another vulture, soaring away across the mountainside.

Stormrider took flight from the branch, flapping after the shadow, afraid that she might lose it. But where was the Great Mother leading her? They seemed to be heading back to the vulture pool, and Stormrider's insides clenched at the idea— that place was still full of the bones and feathers of the dead. She didn't want to go back there.

But the Great Mother's shadow veered away from the pool at the last minute, flying up and up, to the very peak of a high jutting rock farther along the mountain. Stormrider circled it curiously and saw that the flickering shadow alighted on a perch on the rock, and its shape took on the silhouette of a gazelle, long horns pointing toward a small cave in the peak.

Stormrider landed and poked her head inside.

Her heart gave a flutter, and she let out a loud caw of surprise and of joy.

Inside the cave, there was a nest. And inside the nest, a clutch of three large, perfect vulture eggs.

Guard them carefully, said Great Mother's voice.

The shadow faded from sight, and Stormrider hurriedly settled down over the eggs, fussing them, making sure that they were all right. They would hatch any moment now, she was sure. The Great Mother had found them just in time.

"Thank you, Prance," she said.

The voice came one last time, a whisper of a laugh on the wind that whistled around the high peak.

They are the future, she said.

And under her feathers, Stormrider began to feel a movement, something tapping with a new, soft beak on the inside of an egg.

She settled down, laying her head close to the egg that was shifting beneath her.

"Let me tell you a story," she said. "It's almost the oldest story, and it begins with an egg. . . ."